GRIMSTONE

A CROFT & WESSON ADVENTURE

BRAD MAGNARELLA

Copyright © 2017 and 2021 by Brad Magnarella

All rights reserved.

No part of this book may be reproduced in any form or by any electronic or mechanical means, including information storage and retrieval systems, without written permission from the author, except for the use of brief quotations in a book review.

Cover design by Deranged Doctor Design

bradmagnarella.com

THE PROF CROFT SERIES

PREQUELS
Book of Souls
Siren Call

MAIN SERIES
Demon Moon
Blood Deal
Purge City
Death Mage
Black Luck
Power Game
Druid Bond
Night Rune
Shadow Duel
Shadow Deep
Godly Wars
Angel Doom

SPIN OFFS
Croft & Tabby
Croft & Wesson

MORE COMING!

1

A cold wind batted my trench coat and threw dust into the idling cab's high beams as I approached the double-wide trailer. The cabbie had been nervous about driving out here this late in the day, no doubt for its remoteness—and for whatever came out at night in these parts. Dusk was fast settling over the barren canyon, throwing the rising moon into sharp relief.

"He better be home," I muttered.

The trailer's porch light was broken, but at the far end past a rail slung with jeans, light glowed behind a window's miniblinds. I set my suitcase down and rapped on the door with my cane. When no one answered, I rapped again, louder. Good thing I'd asked the cabbie to wait.

A fit of barking erupted from inside the trailer. Footsteps followed the barking to the door. "Chill out, girl," I heard James saying.

I waved to the cabbie. He tooted the horn and wheeled around, the taillights diminishing down the dirt road in a small storm of dust.

"Prof, you made it!"

I turned back to the sight of James in the doorway, a silver cross dangling over his chest, his smile a shining crescent in his smooth, mahogany-colored face. He had on the same leather vest and cowboy hat I'd last seen him in a few months earlier when we worked together in New York. For a junior wizard, he was fundamentally sound, I'd give him that. But he was also inexperienced. And cocky. No doubt why our magical order had sent me to help him on what they'd described as a challenging case.

Everson Croft, wizard babysitter, I thought wryly.

"Was starting to think you'd decided to stay home," James joked.

I forced a chuckle while picturing myself back in my Manhattan loft apartment, feet up, a steaming mug of Colombian coffee in hand, tome of advanced spells open on my lap. Instead, another magic-user was covering my beat, and I was walking into God only knew what.

"No, no, my plane got delayed in—Jesus!" I cried as a pit bull's black and white head lunged forward.

"Oh, don't worry about Annie," he said, seizing her studded collar at the same moment her teeth snapped an inch from my crotch. "She's a big baby. Go to your bed," he ordered.

Annie glowered up at me, a growl in her throat, before retreating back into the house. I made sure she wasn't returning before relaxing my pelvis forward and accepting James's handshake.

He yanked me into a hug. "Good to see you, bro."

"Yeah, you too," I managed from inside his embrace. Though we were about the same six-foot height, James had a good twenty pounds of muscle on me. He pounded my back twice and released me.

"Here, let me get that," he said, reaching for my suitcase.

I stared at his other hand. "You're drinking a beer?"

James looked from me to the green bottle. "Yeah, want one?"

I pressed my lips together. "You do realize I'm here at the request of the Order, right?"

"Yeah?"

"And the plan was to get started today, the moment I arrived?"

He shrugged. "You're two hours late, man."

My neck tensed, but I managed to control my voice. If I lost it now, it was going to be a long week. "Right, because my plane was delayed. Something I had no control over. I called you from the airport when I landed, but you didn't answer and your voicemail was full."

He screwed up his face in confusion, then broke into dawning laughter. "Oh, yeah, I was shredding on the guitar. Had the amps jacked up to eight. Must not have heard the phone."

"James, the fact that the Order asked me to come should have told you this case is serious. I asked you to be ready. I asked you to lay out everything you had so we could start planning. But because I was late, you decided to, what, crack a few beers and have a jam session?"

"My satellite's out," he said. "Nothing to stream."

"I think you're missing the point. If—"

"Hey, ah, hold that thought, Prof," James interrupted, showing me a hand.

Okay, that did it. No more calm, understanding Everson. But

James was squinting past me, his blue irises picking up bits of light. Beyond the moaning wind came the sound of rumbling engines. I turned toward the sight of a small convoy of pickup trucks jouncing down the dirt drive. Floodlights shone above their high beams. Something told me this wasn't a courtesy call.

"Well, shit," James said.

"Care to fill me in?"

"I might have made a few enemies on the hustling circuit."

"Hustling?" I asked, incredulous. "Here?"

"It gets better, Prof."

"I can't wait to hear how."

"They're sort of werewolves."

I looked from the approaching trucks to James, waiting for the punch line. He shrugged and took another swig of beer.

"I don't frigging believe this," I muttered.

James tossed his bottle aside and reached beneath the flaps of his vest, unhasping a Colt Peacemaker at each hip. The floodlights illuminated his face as the three trucks skidded to a stop in front of the trailer.

He nudged my shoulder. "Did I mention it was good to see you?"

2

For several moments the black trucks idled in a V formation. I raised a hand to shield my eyes from their floodlights, a sour bite of adrenaline growing in my mouth. Annie went into a barking fit. I was about to suggest we'd be safer inside with her, behind the trailer's protective wards, when the truck doors opened.

The nine men who stepped out were stocky, faces and arms tapestries of dark ink. Eight of them spread into a wide semicircle, submachine guns in hand, while a lean man strode forward, thumbs hooked into the belt loops of his black jeans. The trucks backlit his slender ponytail as he peered up at us.

"Señor Wesson," he called, gold glinting from his teeth. Noting the canines, I gripped my cane more tightly.

"Hey. Santana," James said. "What's up?"

"Oh, I think you know what's up."

"'Fraid not. You're going to have to spell it out."

Santana chuckled in a way that said he knew James was only trying to buy himself time. Thick scars curled his lingering smile, making it appear more dangerous. Despite being smaller than the others, and unarmed, Santana was clearly the leader of the pack. The Alpha.

"A couple of weeks ago, you visited one of our establishments," he said, "played a few games of pool. Did well, I understand."

"I did all right," James hedged.

"Oh, I'd say you did better than all right. You won close to five grand, correct?"

I looked back at James.

"Hey, it was a slow week," he whispered.

"Yeah, and that's when you should be studying and training," I whispered back. "Not hustling in pool houses."

"Prof, I need you not to judge me right now."

Santana whistled sharply. "I asked you a question, hijo."

"Yeah, give or take five grand," James allowed.

I noticed that the other werewolves had spread out such that the front and sides of the trailer were now covered. Two had disappeared from view, gone to cover the back door, no doubt. Eyeing the wolves' guns, I called power to my mental prism and readied a shield invocation.

Santana shook his head as he strolled nearer. His white shirt was open at the collar, and the words "LOS LOBOS" had been stenciled across the top of his chest in a way that made it look as if they were dripping blood. So not only were we dealing with werewolves, but one of Latin America's most lethal gangs.

Keeps getting better.

"You know gambling is illegal in Grimstone County?" Santana said. "And when it happens in one of our establishments, we're liable. Happens enough times and we get shut down, put out of business. But hustlers like you gonna hustle, right? We get it. We take on that risk, for your sake." He opened his hands in a gesture of generosity before thrusting up a finger with a thick, blade-like nail. "But at a price. Twenty-five percent of winnings."

James let out an embarrassed laugh that was totally unconvincing. "Oh, man. Can't believe I forgot to settle up. It was late, I'd had a few beers. Yeah, man, if you give me a sec, I'll go get it."

"He didn't come for the twenty-five percent," I muttered.

Santana's preternatural hearing picked up my remark. "Your friend is correct. By ducking out, you forfeited your winnings. All of them. Not only that, but you're now two weeks late. That means interest, hijo. And the rates in our business are—how should I put it?—*aggressive*."

"How much we talking?" James asked.

"You now owe us ten thousand."

"Ten thou? Look, man, I don't have that kind of money lying around. How about I get you the five tonight and we call it even. First offense and all of that? No need to be a hard ass."

I massaged my temples. *James, you ever-loving idiot.*

Santana's smile vanished. "Hard ass? You think this is me being a hard ass?" Muscles rippled up and down his arms as he stalked forward. Thick black hair sprouted from his cheeks and forearms. My gaze shot to his men, who were also beginning to transform. Yellow eyes blazed from the darkness as their guns rose into firing positions. Behind us, Annie's barking climbed an octave, her nails scratching up and down the door.

I watched James take stock of the situation. "Fuck this," he decided. *"Liberare!"*

The air pressure dropped as James channeled a current through himself, down the frame of the front porch, and into the ground. I blurted out my own invocation. White light burst from the opal in my cane and slid into a powerful shield around us, intercepting the incoming gunfire. Explosions began pluming from the front yard, engulfing the wolves.

"Claymores," James shouted proudly as debris from the explosions stormed around us. "I added a little incendiary, a little magic, and buried them around the yard as an outer ring of security."

"Great, but a little warning next time?" I shouted back.

"And you'll be happy to know the mines are packing silver."

A strong wind carried the dust away, revealing the carnage. Shrapnel-torn werewolves writhed on the ground, thick curls of smoke rising from their bodies. The trucks were pitted and their windows smashed. A wolf appeared to have run into one, knocking the truck onto its side.

I dropped my gaze to where Santana had been thrown. The back of his shirt was blown open, and his hairy back was matted with blood. His transformation complete, he struggled up to his legs and raised his face. Bloodied lips peeled back from a protruding jaw to reveal two impressive rows of gold-plated fangs. The amber eyes that met James's burned with murder.

"You're dead, hijo," he snarled.

I seized my cane handle and pulled, releasing a beveled sword with runes down one side. Cutting in front of James, I held out the glowing blade with one hand and what had become a staff with the other. Santana reared back, growling as he eyed the blade's silver edge.

Behind me, James cocked his Peacemakers.

"*Pinche* wizards," Santana seethed, trembling from the pain of the shrapnel.

"That's right," James said. "Two of them."

"Always happy to get involved," I muttered. I looked over at where my suitcase had been blown from the porch, its contents strewn across the yard. My favorite shirt was on fire.

But I remained alert for the two who had disappeared behind the trailer. In a sudden motion, gunfire flashed to either side of us. As lines of sparks stitched my shield, I thrust my sword and staff out.

"*Vigore!*" I shouted.

Bright pulses shot from each, smashing the weapons from the werewolves' grips. James followed up, firing with both guns. The wolves recoiled, hairy chunks of tissue blowing from their bodies.

"Yee-haw!" he cried, working the hammers with his thumbs. Considering the circumstances, he was enjoying himself way too much.

The distraction gave Santana an opening. With a roar, he sprang up the porch steps. The energy it had taken me to cast dual invocations had weakened my shield, and the werewolf's impact finished it.

The shield failed in a bright curtain of sparks, throwing me backwards. I landed against the trailer door, which James's pit bull was still trying to claw her way through. Heart slamming, I thrust my sword up into a blocking position, but James came to my defense first, standing nose to snout with Santana, the barrels of his Peacemakers pressed to the Alpha's chest.

"So much as twitch and I'll empty them into your heart," James said.

"Better make sure you kill me, *hijo*," Santana growled, still trembling from the shrapnel inside him.

"With .45 silver composites? Not a problem."

"No one's killing anyone!"

I turned toward the harsh voice. A short, gray-haired woman was limping around the toppled truck and past the downed wolves, a bolt-action rifle aimed at the porch. By the mechanical way in which her left leg swung, I guessed she was wearing a prosthesis beneath her slacks.

"What now?" I groaned.

"You see what this punk did to my men?" Santana demanded, eyes still locked on James's.

"I'm not blind," the woman answered. "Looks an awful lot like self-defense."

"Thank you," James said, his revolvers still pressing into Santana.

"And stupidity," she added, directing that comment at James. "On the count of three, you're going to back away from each other, or I'll take you both down." The woman arrived to one side of the porch steps, the rifle steady at her shoulder. "One ... two ..."

With a hard sigh, James eased back. When Santana didn't come after him, he lowered the Peacemakers.

"You," the woman said to Santana. "Off the porch."

She gestured with her weapon, but Santana remained glaring at James, nostrils flaring, foam frothing around his gold fangs with each harsh breath.

"Now!" the woman shouted.

"This ain't over, hijo," Santana whispered to James.

Melding back into his human form, he sauntered down the steps. The silver in the shrapnel had stunted his regenerative abilities, but he was healing, his body pushing the shards from his back. They dropped to the ground behind him. The other wolves struggled to their feet and reclaimed their weapons. Two of them staggered to the toppled truck and hefted it upright.

The woman tracked them with her rifle as they climbed inside their vehicles. Engines roared. As Santana's truck passed us, he aimed his first two fingers from the broken passenger window and mimed shooting James, then me. His gold fangs flashed in a final grin, and the trucks swung away.

The woman watched them for a moment, then lowered the rifle to one hand. She limped up the steps.

James straightened his hat. "Damn, Marge. Nice timing."

"Shut up," she snapped. She was a head shorter than both of us, her face lean and leathery from what looked like a lifetime in the arid climate. She squinted up at me with salty blue eyes.

"You him?" she demanded.

"Um, I'm not sure. My name's Everson Croft. And you are...?"

"Didn't bother telling him I was coming, huh?" the woman asked James. She sighed and lifted one side of her open jacket to reveal a star-shaped badge on the pocket of her shirt. "Sheriff Jackson," she said. "Now get your asses inside. We've got work to do."

3

Ten minutes later the three of us—James, Sheriff Jackson, and I—were sitting around a small dining-room table. Sheriff Jackson, who was easier for me to think of as Marge, had returned to her truck to retrieve a stack of thick manila files. She was one of those people you either immediately liked or disliked. I liked her—not only because she seemed to have James's number, but when Annie growled menacingly, Marge thumped her nose, sending the dog away, whimpering.

"Missing persons files," Marge said, patting the stack. "Eight of them. All young women between the ages of twenty-two and twenty-six. All blond-haired. And all within the last year."

I pulled a small spiral notepad from an inside coat pocket and jotted down the information. "And you think the cause is supernatural?"

"I wouldn't have contacted Mr. Wesson here if I didn't. Believe me." She cut her gaze to my partner in a way that suggested they'd butted heads. Only six months out here and James had already managed to piss off the law.

"Theories on the disappearances?" I asked James.

"Theories?" he repeated. "The second Marge came to me, the Order called and told me to hold off, that they were going to send you out to hold my hand. I know about as much as you do. Not that I'm complaining. All my work so far has been in the New Age communes, especially the ones into sprites and fairies. They've been calling up all kinds of crap I've had to put down."

This region of western Colorado featured wild patterns of ley energy. Attempts at magic, especially summonings by novice practitioners, would lead to exactly what James described—the appearance of nether creatures. No doubt why he'd been assigned out here.

"How about the sheriff's department, then?" I asked Marge. "Any leads?"

"Well, young women up and leaving isn't unheard of in Grimstone County," she said. "We're not exactly overflowing with job opportunities. But the pattern of the disappearances tells me the women were targeted. For their age, their looks, their ease of access, maybe. All the women lived alone."

"No husbands or significant others?" I asked.

"A few had boyfriends," Marge said. "But interviews and searches didn't turn up anything suspicious. A couple of the boyfriends did think they were being unfaithful, though."

"Why?" I asked.

"Said their girls had received gifts before they disappeared. Gold bracelets."

"Anything I can take a look at?"

The jewelry, with its bonding energy between giver and receiver, would make a potent target for a hunting spell. But when I glanced up from my notepad, Marge was shaking her head.

"Girls must've been wearing the bracelets when they disappeared because we didn't find anything. And their secret admirers didn't call or text. There was nothing in their phone records."

I rested my chin on a fist. Had the young women been lured by someone or something? A vampire, maybe? I turned back to James.

"What can you tell me about the supernatural geography of Grimstone County?"

Not expecting much, I was surprised when he grinned and stood. "I think you'll be proud of me, Prof." He disappeared into his bedroom and returned a moment later with a large, rolled-up piece of paper. He pulled off a rubber band and spread the paper across the table displaying a map of Grimstone County onto which he'd made notations using colored pens.

"The area's best understood in quadrants," he said, standing over my right shoulder and indicating the two highways that formed a cross in approximately the center of the map. "The southeast quadrant features the town of Grimstone, surrounded by miles of Hicklandia."

"Watch your mouth," Marge said. "I grew up on a ranch in what you call 'Hicklandia.'"

"There are a few wandering currents of ley energy," James went on, tracing the blue lines he'd drawn. "Most terminate around the New Age communes. We're over here, in this canyon."

I'd wondered why the Order had picked somewhere so remote to stick James. The nexus of ley lines explained it. It gave James a nice wellspring to draw from for spell-casting, though I was going to need to talk to him about his defensive wards. They were sturdy but not solid.

James moved his finger north. "Up here is reservation land, and there's some seriously powerful energy flow. Some of it's natural, but a lot of it's been cultivated by the tribe that inhabits the land."

"Utes," Marge said.

"Ever had any problems with them?" I asked.

Marge shook her head. "They keep themselves to themselves. Don't want much to do with us."

"But there are shifters among them," James said.

"Shifters?" I repeated.

"I saw some of their tribe at the farmer's market one Saturday," he said. "About half a dozen of them, selling rugs, herbal remedies. Tried to see what I could pick up. On the surface, the men and women looked normal, but in their ethereal layers I was seeing all kinds of forms: coyote, crow, snake."

I had to give James credit. He'd been doing some actual work.

"And they *knew* I could see them," James went on. "Their medicine man, this dude with braided white hair, stared right at me like the crowd between us didn't exist. And I swear to God, for a second, my power died. I was defenseless. Couldn't have manifested a flicker of magic if I'd tried. When he broke eye contact, my power came back, but it was like he'd issued a warning. 'Stay out of my business, and I'll stay out of yours.'" James removed his hat and ran a hand over his pile of hair. "I hope to hell they're not involved in this."

Outside, the wind banged the screen door, and a den of coyotes yipped in the distance. "Could one of theirs have— excuse the pun—gone off the reservation?" I asked Marge.

"It happens," she answered. "But they discipline their own real quick. A few years back, we had a slew of car jackings. Never caught the perp, but at about the time the jackings stopped, one of the teenagers in the tribe was seen walking around in a wooden stockade, portable. Wore it for about a month."

"A month?" I said. "Is that even legal?"

Marge shrugged. "Not my jurisdiction. Belongs to the Bureau of Indian Affairs, which hardly ever comes around anymore. That's the thing. When the economy went tits up and federal budgets got slashed, the treaty that protects that particular reservation stopped looking so bulletproof. Some potential loopholes in there, apparently, and the Utes don't want to give anyone an excuse to exploit them. All kinds of interests looking to get their hands on that land."

"Such as?"

"Mining, for one," she said. "The gold claims in Grimstone County are all dug out. Speculators think the Utes are sitting on a rich vein. Water rights for another. The Dolores River flows right through the middle of Ute land. Then there are the developers. Brunhold Development runs the show in Grimstone County. They've talked about building a huge golf-course community up there—something to lure the wealthy from the ski-slope towns in the summer."

I nodded, but we were getting off topic. "So if the perp had been one of their own, the tribe would have nipped it in the bud."

"A long time ago," Marge assured me.

James nodded solemnly, no doubt still dwelling on the power the medicine man had wielded over him.

"What's all of this up here?" I asked, indicating the northeast quadrant.

"Grimstone County is a hub for trucking because of the exchange," Marge said. "Everything a trucker could want is located within a one-mile radius: filling stations, repair shops, diners, motels."

James coughed into a fist. "Special services."

"What, like drugs and prostitution?" I asked.

"Hey, it's a problem anywhere there's trucking," Marge said defensively. "We keep tabs on it."

"Attracts some nasty creatures, though," James said. "Those wolves you met earlier? Santana and his gang are out of Honduras. They run some legit businesses, but their main commerce is drug shipping."

"Legit businesses like pool halls?" I asked thinly.

James looked from me to Marge and back in a way that said, *Can we talk about that later?*

I shook my head wearily. "All right, we've got the town, ranchland, and communes down here, reservation land up here, trucking services over here. What about this?" I asked, tapping the final quadrant in the southwest. The area was brown, a few dotted lines signifying dirt roads.

"The old mining land I mentioned," Marge said. "Nothing much there now."

My gaze lingered on the barren quadrant before I took in the whole map again. "Can you show me where the disappearances happened?"

Marge rotated the map until it was in front of her, drew a pen from a breast pocket, and, consulting her files, began making notations: names, dates, and the order of each disappearance. When she rotated the map back to me, I noticed that the majority of disappearances had happened in town. Two had occurred in the ranches around town and one more in the trucking district. In fact, the trucking-district disappearance had been the first.

"A lot lizard," Marge said, following my gaze.

I felt my brow crease in question. "Lot lizard?"

"A prostitute who works the trucking lots," she explained, pulling a photo from one of the files and placing it on the map. It was a headshot of the missing girl from what looked like a prior arrest. She was sallow-faced and tragically young, her blond hair hanging in damp crimps.

I read her name aloud. "Dawn Michaels."

"We'd never have known she'd disappeared if a trucker hadn't reported her missing," Marge said. "He was an older man, apparently sweet on her. We figured Dawn had moved on, but when we interviewed friends, we learned she'd never talked about leaving. She just up and disappeared. At first we suspected a long-haul trucker, but when the disappearances shifted to the town, we started thinking it was the work of a local."

"And no leads?"

Marge was placing the photos of the remaining girls on the map, a couple of the photos cheap-looking glamour shots. "Not yet," she said.

"So what makes you think the perp is a supernatural?" I asked.

"I've seen enough in my career to know when I'm dealing with a human and when I'm dealing with an Other, as I call them. Humans leave evidence. In these cases, there hasn't been shit. Whatever's making off with the blondes comes and goes like a fart in the wind. My gut's saying Other."

I nodded. My gut was saying Other too. "Are the girls all natural blondes?"

"Does it matter?" Marge asked.

"It might."

"I'll find out then."

I nodded and looked over the map again, studying the headshots of each of the disappeared women. "So, with the first victim, the perp must have been going after the low-hanging fruit. A girl in that occupation would be easy to get alone, I'm guessing. Wouldn't be missed right away, and wouldn't necessarily be a priority for law enforcement. No offense."

"None taken, but I wouldn't call the lot lizards low-hanging fruit," Marge said. "Not with Helga looking after them."

"Is she their pimp?" I asked.

"Their *madam*," Marge said. "Or matron, as she prefers to be called."

"And she also happens to be a major witch," James put in.

"That's witch with a 'w,' right?"

"With a 'b' too," Marge muttered. "She's been no help in the investigation. We were only able to talk to a few of the girls before she silenced them. She insisted that all communications go through her. 'Course she wasn't talking, either. Just said no one knew anything."

"Do you think Helga has something to do with this?" I asked, jotting down the name.

"Maybe not directly, but she knows more than she's letting on," Marge said. "I'd start there."

"So it's all right if we talk to her?" I asked carefully. Marge seemed open to James's and my line of work—a rarity in law enforcement—but there remained the touchy subject of jurisdiction. She hadn't invited us to look at the case files and was only doling out info piecemeal. As consultants, I wasn't sure how far she would allow us to venture onto her turf.

"If it were just Wesson here, I'd mind," she replied. "But you seem to know your shit."

James frowned. "That hurts, Marge."

She ignored him, her eyes narrowing in on mine. "But I'm still the law out here. I want you checking in at every step. You don't so much as glance at a suspect or witness without my say-so. And that goes double for your partner. He might be a crack wizard, and damned handsome, but he's trouble."

"I'll take the handsome part," James said. "But trouble?"

"Understood," I assured her. "And I'll keep him in line."

Marge searched my eyes another moment—I sensed she was good at reading people—then gave a grudging nod. I'd passed her test, but I was going to have to tread really carefully.

"Anything I can be doing?" she asked.

"Actually, there is," I said. "If you could get me a few items that belonged to the missing girls, I'll attempt a hunting spell. We may be able to track them down that way."

Or their remains, I thought grimly.

"I'll see what I can do." Marge scooted her chair from the table and stood. She gathered up the files and began limping toward the door. When Annie started to rise from her dog bed, Marge narrowed her eyes at her. The dog licked her muzzle with a whimper and lowered herself back down.

"How much time do we have?" James asked.

It was actually a good question. I glanced over the dates again, then looked up at Marge, who had stopped at the door. "Disappearances are happening about twenty-nine days apart," she said. "Sometimes a little less, sometimes a little more."

"Wait," I said, doing the math. "That only gives us..."

"One day," Marge finished for me. "Give or take."

In the living room, James removed the cushions from a beat-up sofa and pulled out the sleeper. After Marge's visit, I'd put him to work making some potions we might need while I attuned myself to the patterns of ley energy in the area and calibrated my sword and staff. It was almost midnight now.

"I'll be honest," James said, yawning. "I bitched when the Order told me to wait for you, but it's good to see you again. I'm glad you're here."

I eyed the thin, yellow-stained mattress sprinkled with dog hair. "Yeah..."

"I've got some spare sheets somewhere." James's upper body disappeared into an overstuffed closet. After digging around, he pulled out a balled-up fitted sheet and ragged orange comforter. A couple moths scattered from the second and beat around the room's ceiling light.

"Don't bother," I said. "I can use my coat."

"What kind of host would that make me?"

"A merciful one?"

But James didn't hear me. He was tossing the sheet and comforter into the air and thrusting his wand toward them. *"Limpiare!"* he called.

Silver light flashed from the end of the wand and infused the bedding, suspending it in midair. When the silver light faded, the sheet and comforter looked pristine, straight out of packaging. With a force invocation and subtle twists of his wand, James tucked the bedding around the mattress and even fluffed a mismatched pair of pillows, which he set at the head.

"Not bad," I allowed, sitting on the side of the bed to untie my shoes. "Looks like you're keeping up your magic when you're not too busy stiffing werewolf gangsters."

"C'mon, man. I told you, it was just that one time."

"Tell it to Santana."

James sighed. "I screwed up, all right? I'll handle it."

"How?"

"I'll pay him the money."

I stopped removing my shoes and stared at him.

"What?" he asked.

"James, you just challenged the Alpha in front of his pack. Money or not—and I don't even want to know how you're planning to get ten thousand—he's not walking away from this. He *can't* walk away from this. It's in his DNA. You understand that, don't you?"

James rubbed the back of his neck. "I considered that."

"Before or after you tried to blow him up?"

"Look, man. What's done is done. I'm sorry for getting you involved, but it won't affect our work on the case. I promise."

"How can you promise something you have no control over?"

"You met Marge, man. You saw how she operates."

"Yeah?"

"Well, Santana might be a bad mother, but he's smart. He knows that if he wants to keep doing business in Grimstone, he needs to stay off Marge's radar. Her rolling up on him in the middle of a shakedown doesn't exactly further his cause. He's got no choice but to lay low. He'll come at me again, yeah, but you'll be long gone when that happens. The case will be in the bag."

"Not if the case involves the wolves."

"The wolves? Based on what?"

"Did you notice anything about the dates of the disappearances?"

"Besides them being a month apart?" A look of understanding came over his face and he peeked out the blinds. The large moon shone above the near wall of the canyon. "Oh, shit."

"Yeah, they're coinciding with the moon cycle. And we're one night from full."

He let the blinds snap closed. "You think Santana is behind it?"

"Or one of his pack, maybe. But let's get some rest and see what the witch can tell us in the morning."

4

I woke up to bright sunlight streaming through the mini blinds. After pawing around for my watch, I checked the time.

Quarter till ten. Crap, I'd overslept!

I dressed quickly and headed to James's room to wake him up, but the bed was empty. In the kitchen, a pot of coffee sat in a cheap coffee maker. When I heard a car door slam, I walked out the back door. Annie barked from a chain in the middle of a yard that featured a clothes line, an old septic tank, and a lot of dirt. I watched from the back porch as James loaded the rear of a black Jeep. He was wearing his cowboy hat and a matching pair of steel-toed boots.

"No horse?" I asked.

James looked over. "Hey, Prof. Sleep all right?"

"Too well, apparently." I descended the steps. "Why didn't you wake me?"

"You looked shot last night. Thought an extra hour or two would do you good."

As I approached the Jeep, I saw that his cargo was a small

arsenal he was loading into a custom compartment. The weapons looked vintage. A Winchester pump-action shotgun was racked vertically beside a pair of lever-action rifles. Cases of ammo lined the other side.

The Colt .45 Peacemakers he'd wielded last night were at his hips, their grips peeking from the flaps of his vest. By coming out West, James's fantasy of being a cowboy had turned into a full-time hobby.

"I didn't realize we were going to the O.K. Corral," I said.

"Joke all you want, but these have gotten me out of some serious pinches."

"Do I even want to hear about them?"

"Probably not."

I considered the arsenal. "You do understand this is just an interview, right?"

"Yeah, with an extremely moody witch."

"A *matron* witch," I stressed. "And that's not just an honorific, as Sheriff Jackson seems to think. It means she's powerful. The only hope we have of getting her help is by ass-kissing, not showing up with a small gunroom and tough talk. Probably why she didn't cooperate with the sheriff."

"Fine, we'll keep the big guns on standby."

I nodded at his holster. "The revolvers too. Your wand will suffice."

Annie's barking continued unabated as James relented and stored the Peacemakers beside the guns and ammo, locked the compartment, and slammed the Jeep's rear door.

"Anything else, Prof?"

"We'll need to bring Helga a gift."

"What kind of gift?" he asked.

"First, what can you tell me about her?"

As James drove, he shared what he knew about Helga, shouting to be heard over the roar of gravel and wind. It wasn't the way I'd envisioned planning our interview with the witch, but I'd overslept and, with only one day until another disappearance, we were short on time.

"According to the records, Helga emigrated from Russia with her two sisters," James said. "Showed up in Grimstone County in the mid eighteen hundreds. They opened Grimstone's first saloon-slash-brothel. There was a gold rush around that time. The town was also on a trade route, so business was good. Competing saloons came and went, but not theirs."

"Pays to be a spell-caster," I said.

"Well, at least until the Depression hit. Happened about the same time the mines were drying up. The saloon lost clients as people left town. Then, in the late thirties, Helga's two sisters died under mysterious circumstances."

"I'll bet," I said. "With money tight, she no doubt offed her business partners. Witches can be ruthless that way."

"Helga managed to keep the saloon going until the economy recovered. And when the major highways were built in the fifties, it was boom time again. By then, Helga had turned the saloon into a full-blown hotel. Pretty nice one, too. Grimstone is one of the most prized routes in the long-haul trucking game. Drivers will actually fight one another for a run through this part of the state, all so they can stay at Helga's hotel or park in one of the lots she services. It's weird. I mean, her women aren't exactly top shelf."

"Then her magic must be," I said.

"Guess so. There was a story going around soon after I got

here. Apparently, a trucker mistreated one of her girls—this big dude everyone called Rip. Helga turned Rip into a slug."

"An actual slug?"

"It happened over a few weeks. First his skin turned gray and wet, and then this putrid smell started coming off him, like rotting meat. His wife was so repulsed, she left him. Took the kids. Not long after, Rip had to be put in a nursing home. Needed total care. When a trucker friend of his went to visit, Rip insisted he keep the light off. All the friend could make out was a shapeless mound that squelched every time it shifted. After a couple of minutes, the smell drove the friend away, but not before Rip managed to tell him Helga had cursed him in a dream. Word spread through the trucking networks. Apparently, Helga makes an example of jerks like Rip every few years, and it works. Helga's girls are treated like royalty."

"Wonder how Dawn got plucked, then." Helga obviously hadn't done anything punitive because the perp struck seven more times. Of course, Helga could also have been behind it.

James shrugged. "Beats me. Hey, uh, that thing with the wolves last night... That doesn't have to get back to the Order, does it?"

"Depends."

"On what?"

"On how the next few days go. We're going to be working this case. Not drinking beers, not shooting pool, not chasing skirts. If you can show me that you're taking this seriously, and if there are no more surprises from your few months in Grimstone, then no. What happened last night doesn't have to get back to the Order."

"You're a good man," he said.

I grunted and took a sip of the coffee he'd poured into a

thermos for me. It was cold and watery. I drank it anyway, if only for the caffeine.

"So, what have you been up to, Prof?" The "Prof" referred to my position at Midtown College in Manhattan, where I was a professor of ancient mythology and lore. By day, anyway.

I wiped my mouth and put the thermos away. "Same as you, I imagine. Tracking down summoned creatures, banishing them to their realms, sealing the holes behind them." Lately, the cases had been coming in bunches, and I was chronically exhausted. Little wonder I'd overslept.

"The Order wasn't kidding," James said. "Things have definitely gotten stranger."

"No thanks to the Whisperer," I muttered.

"So how long is our world going to stay porous?"

"As long as it takes for the senior members of the Order to stitch up the holes."

"And how long's that going to be?"

"Your guess is as good as mine. But with the Order tied up, we're on our own out here." I let that hang between us, hoping it would sink in. But James only nodded vaguely and snapped on the car stereo. An electric guitar wailed from the speakers. I snapped it back off.

"What does Helga look like?" I asked.

"Big."

"That's it?"

"It's the first thing that comes to mind. You'll see what I mean."

"I think I know what to get her, then. Is there a butcher in town?"

Helga's hotel rose like a mirage amid the gritty trucking lots and warehouses. Its pale blue façade with gold-topped columns, tall windows, and ornate balconies gave it the look of a Russian palace.

"That *is* nice," I said as we pulled into the front lot. According to James, Helga had two stables of women: those who worked in the hotel and those who worked the lots beside the exchange. Dawn Michaels had belonged to the second.

"And well-guarded," James remarked.

"Huh?" I followed his gaze to the front of the hotel but didn't see anything.

"The astral plane?" he prompted.

"Oh, right." Embarrassment prickled my face as I opened my senses. And here I was supposed to be the more experienced one. It took a moment for the hotel and its surroundings to shift to a plane of humming energies. There was magic at work here. Not evil magic, necessarily, but dark enough. It wrapped the hotel like steam from a cauldron. And then I spotted them: imps.

I sighed as I watched the creatures flap around the hotel on tattered wings, their bony bodies trailing tendrils of black smoke.

I hated imps.

"Should I grab the shotgun?" James asked. "I've got a case of rock-salt shells."

"No, let's stick to the plan." I gripped my cane and the large white box from the butcher's shop and got out of the Jeep. "Just let me do the talking."

James shrugged and joined me at the front of the Jeep. We were halfway across the lot when the imps began turning their stick-like noses toward us. A screech of warning went up. They sensed our magic. Two flew into the hotel, likely to warn Helga, while the rest raced toward us. When James reached into a vest pocket for his wand, I shook my head.

"Keep cool," I whispered.

James's jaw tensed as he lowered his arm. Within moments we were surrounded, the pigeon-sized imps flapping around us, poking and prodding our pockets, all while beclouding the air with their sulfurous stink.

One snatched James's metal wand from inside his vest. The imp shook it a few times and chattered at the others in a strange tongue. Another imp wrenched my cane from my grip. I had to restrain myself from reaching for it. Two more imps plucked strands of hair off my head while a third squeezed my nose until my eyes began to water.

I noticed James, who was receiving similar treatment, balling up his fists. I got his attention and patted my free hand toward the ground. If either of us retaliated, the devilish creatures would deny our passage.

At last, the imps released us and backed away. I blinked my eyes clear and saw that they had emptied my pockets of spell items and, in James's case, a nickel-plated Derringer. My coin pendant and James's crucifix had been removed from around our necks as well. The imp holding James's wand hovered in front of us. His contemptuous face looked from James to me.

"What's your business, *wizards?*"

"We've come to talk to Helga," I answered.

"About *what?*"

"To introduce ourselves, mainly," I lied. "We've heard stories of Helga's power, and as fellow practitioners of the magical arts, it would be an honor to have an audience with her, however brief."

The way to a matron's shriveled heart was generally through shameless prostration.

"Fellow practitioners," the imp sneered. "As if you're anywhere close to Madam Helga's equal."

"No, no," I said quickly to cover up James's derisive snort. "I didn't mean it in that way, I assure you. We are but simple magic-users. James here can hardly heat a pot of water. "

The imps elbowed one another and snickered. But the lead imp continued to regard us with suspicion. "If you two are so pathetic, why should you be granted an audience with Madam Helga?" he asked.

I held up the butcher box, which was now dripping blood. "We bring a gift."

Several of the imps had poked the box, but sensing no magic or danger, they'd left it alone. Now the lead imp peeked inside. He eyed us with even more suspicion, then said something to an imp beside him. In a streak of smoke, the imp zipped toward the hotel.

The lead imp remained in front of us, bony arms crossed. Behind him, another imp was pretending to sword-fight with my cane. I watched nervously. The blade and staff were my most powerful items. At last, the imp who had gone into the hotel returned and whispered into the imp leader's pointed ear. The leader grunted in response, looking disappointed. A promising sign.

"Helga will see you now," he muttered.

"My wand?" James said, ignoring my instructions about letting me do the talking.

The imp jerked the wand out of James's reach and slapped his hand down. "After the meeting," he said sharply. "Same goes for your cane," he told me, snatching it from the sword-fighting imp.

I was debating whether or not to back out of the meeting —we were all but defenseless—when I spotted my mother's emo ball. A pair of imps were tossing the tennis-ball-sized orb back and forth. I cringed as one nearly fumbled it.

When the lead imp turned to order the creatures back to their patrols, I directed my wizard's voice at one of the imps playing catch.

"Hey, toss it here," I whispered.

The vocal power compelled the simple creature. Without hesitating, he underhanded the emo ball to me. I caught it and slipped it into a coat pocket right before the lead imp turned back toward us.

He grunted and waved for James and me to follow him to the front doors of the hotel.

The marble lobby featured a bar at one end, where young women in short leather skirts and crop tops lounged on couches, waiting for clients. Seductive enchantments swirled around them. I caught James staring at their offerings. My own gaze went to their wrists, remembering what Sheriff Jackson had said about some of the disappeared women receiving gifts of bracelets. The girls glanced up at us blandly before returning their faces to their smartphones.

"This way," the imp snapped.

He was hovering inside one of the elevators, and James and I got in beside him. As the door closed and the elevator lifted off, I noticed the imp eyeing the bloody butcher's box hungrily. A narrow tongue darted over his gray lips, but the gift was for his master. I just hoped she would be as eager for it as he was.

The elevator door opened onto a large penthouse, and we stepped into another century. Thick red drapes swooped down from the room's tall windows. Paintings of Russian royalty hung above antique chairs and couches. A giant chandelier made of gold and crystal seemed to spread from the ceiling. But despite the expensive décor, the room smelled swampy.

"Take off your shoes," someone said in a thick Russian accent.

Beneath the far window, a woman reclined on a divan. I recognized Helga by James's one-word description: big. The gold-embroidered gown she wore barely contained her bean-bag sized breasts while the bones in her bodice appeared ready to crack. We were talking six, seven hundred pounds, easy. As she waved a hand toward our feet, the flesh beneath her arm jiggled.

"Your shoes," she repeated.

As James and I stooped down to pull our shoes off, I whispered, "There are protocols for addressing a matron witch. Let me handle the formalities. Not a word out of you."

"Got it, chief," he whispered back.

We straightened at the same time. Helga regarded us coldly, her gray eyes at odds with the colorful feathers in her piles of thick black hair. From a powder-covered face, her eyes narrowed.

"Matron Helga," I began. "It is an exquisite honor to—"

"What is in the box?" she interrupted.

"Oh, it is a gift for you, most powerful one."

"Bring it here," she snapped at the imp.

He took the box from my hands and flew it over to Helga.

"Open it," she ordered.

The imp peeled back the lid to reveal a box stuffed with raw sheep hearts, intestines, and other innards. Bowing his head, the imp held the offering toward his master. Her hairy nostrils trembled over the box. Grunting, she lifted out a dripping length of intestine and held it above her open mouth. Her multiple chins convulsed as she gobbled it down like a bird consuming a giant worm.

She wiped her mouth with the back of a hand. "It is disgusting," she declared.

It took me a moment to realize that was a compliment. "I'm honored our humble gift satisfies you, Matron."

The imp continued to flap in place, holding the open box. Helga grunted as she plucked out a stomach sac and bit it in half. The smell was almost worse than the sight of it bursting open. James groaned. I elbowed him in the side and remained facing Helga, a smile fixed on my face.

When Helga had had enough, she waved for the imp to take the box away.

"Now," she said, licking her fingers. "What brings you to me?"

"First, allow us to introduce ourselves. I am Everson Croft, and this is James Wesson." James took the cue, and we both bowed low. "We are humble wizards who have heard of your enormous, um, powers. It is an honor to stand in your presence, though we are admittedly frightened."

A small smile turned up the corners of Helga's wet lips.

So far, so good, I thought. *But this is where it gets tricky.*

"You asked why we have come," I went on. "We hope this does not sound presumptuous, but we seek your wisdom."

"In what matter?" Helga snapped, her smile disappearing.

"In the matter of the young women who have disappeared in the past year." I said carefully, hoping the gift and decorum had done their jobs. If not, James and I were about to witness a very angry witch.

"The young women who have disappeared," she repeated coldly.

"Um, yes, Matron." Beneath my shirt, sweat rolled down the slats of my ribs.

Helga stared at us, her eyes impossible to read. There was nothing to do but await her decision: assist us or cast us out. When a minute passed, James shifted impatiently. Standing around wasn't his thing.

At last he sighed. "The first girl was one of yours."

I looked over at him incredulously. "What the hell are you doing?" I whispered.

"We just want to know what you know," he went on. "We're here to help."

I palmed my face. James's forwardness notwithstanding, you never offered to *help* a matron witch. It was an insult. The worst kind. It was worse than if he'd walked up to her, called her "Fatty," and then spit in her face for good measure. I peeked out between my fingers.

Helga was sitting upright, her great chest heaving, eyes smoldering red. She bared her teeth—iron teeth, I realized—and ground them together. Sparks flashed from her mouth as she stood.

"No, no," I said quickly. "What James meant to say was that we're here to *request* your help, and to request it most humbly, your great, um, matronly one." I threw myself on the ground in prostration, tugging on James's pant leg to do the same. He lowered himself grudgingly, but the damage was already done.

The room darkened, and astral storm winds began tearing around us. I tried to push myself from the floor, but a powerful domination spell pinned me. I could hear James straining beside me. We cycled through our repertoire of invocations, but without my cane or his wand to channel energy, the efforts were too weak to overcome her potent magic.

"You dare offer Madam Helga your *help?*" she shouted from the center of the maelstrom.

When she twisted her long fingernails in front of her, spectral talons raked the length of my back, spilling hot blood down my sides. The pain! My arms buckled, then collapsed. With the next raking, I felt the fibers of my back muscles rip open. She was flaying us alive.

"Keep your help," she screeched. "I will take your pathetic lives instead!"

Outside the windows, the giggling imps crowded against the glass.

5

The next rake of the invisible talons scraped over my vertebrae and the backs of my ribs. Beside me, James released an inhuman grunt. The pain was beyond unbearable. I gnashed my teeth as I tried to twist away.

Helga began to laugh, an awful, guttural sound that shook her flesh.

That ignited a grain of anger inside me. Being done in by a morbidly obese witch was one thing, but I'd be damned if I was going to let her stand in front of us and enjoy it. I couldn't channel enough power to break her hold over us, no. But I had my mother's emo ball.

I wormed my fingers into my coat pocket until the tips encountered glass. With the contact, a warm sensation tingled up my arm. I grasped the enchanted object, and the warmth spread throughout my body, thinning the pain. The witch's laughter faltered.

I pushed myself up to a kneeling position. Helga's face scrunched up as she redoubled her efforts, cheeks reddening beneath the white powder. More sparks flashed from her mouth.

"As a matron witch, you are powerful." I said. "But your power is ineffective over the virtuous, the pure of heart, and"—the emo ball glowed white as I held it out—"those protected by a mother's blessing. And there are few blessings more concentrated than this one."

The love for me that my mother had instilled in the ball pulsed brightly.

Helga looked from the ball to me and James, then let out her breath in an exhausted huff. She sat heavily on the divan, her magic spent.

I let out my own breath, but there was still the matter of our wounds. With my free hand, I touched my back, afraid of what I'd feel. My coat wasn't in bloody shreds. It was intact, along with the skin, muscle, and bone beneath. James appeared to be coming to the same conclusion about himself. Helga had hit us with an enchantment meant to inflict pain and the terror of impending death, but we were unharmed.

"Bolwig," she called. "Fan me."

The lead imp reappeared with a frond-like fan, which he proceeded to wave above her. She pressed the back of a hand to her brow and sighed beneath the gusts of air, her mascara-caked eyelids fluttering closed.

James aimed his eyes toward the elevator as though to say, *Let's get the hell out of here.*

"I will tell you what you want to know," the witch said suddenly.

I looked over at her in surprise. "Yes, Madam Helga?"

"But on two conditions. One, you will tell no one outside of the law, for that is who you are working for, yes? And two, you will agree to complete a task for me at a time of my choosing."

Everything I'd ever read on witches warned against making bargains with them. They were notorious for changing the terms, which were weighted in their favor to begin with. And the tasks were often nefarious. Who knew what Helga had in mind for us. I swore at the turn of events. We were going to have to look for a lead into the disappearances elsewhere.

"We agree," James said.

I whipped my head toward him. He gave me a reassuring nod that did *not* do its job.

"But on the condition that only I perform the task," he continued, "not Everson. You see, Everson doesn't live in Grimstone."

"Very well," Helga replied tiredly.

I had expected her to balk, but the effort of casting against the power of my mother's orb had taken the starch out of her. James grinned at me. The poor bastard had no idea what he was signing up for.

Helga shifted her great bulk on the divan and hacked into her fist. "The girls I employ here are my babies. I take them in. I shelter and protect them. I love them one and all. When my precious Dawn was stolen, it was like someone had torn her from my own womb." Helga held her vast belly and let out a dramatic sob. "I was sad, yes, but also furious that someone would dare steal her. You do not take from Helga."

I nodded, remembering the story about the trucker she'd turned into a slug.

"With the Eye of Baba, I searched for her."

"I'm sorry to interrupt," I said. "But the 'Eye of Baba'?"

Helga dug a hand between her breasts and emerged with

a round pendant that hung from a necklace. At first glance, it looked like a giant pearl that had begun to yellow. But when she rolled it between her fingers, I realized it was a glazed eyeball. She aimed the staring pupil at us.

"The Eye of Baba sees all," she said. "Through it, I can reach anyone, even in his dreams. With the Eye, I looked for Dawn. I looked for the one who had taken her. And when I found them..." Her breaths caught in her chest and her great body began to shudder. The imp fanned faster.

"What?" I asked, unable to help myself. "What happened?"

"I was strangled," she said, gripping her throat while she continued to pant. "By a great and evil power."

"Could you tell what it was?"

"I felt only greed, like a bottomless pit. I cast a dread spell through the Eye, but the greed swallowed it. I then put all my strength into an inflict spell, to injure it. It was just enough. The being released me." Helga unclenched her throat and her breathing normalized. "It was the first time the Eye of Baba had ever failed me," she finished, stuffing it back between her breasts.

"So we're talking about something powerful," James said.

Helga ignored James's very obvious observation. I understood now why she hadn't wanted to talk to the sheriff's department. Her business was built on her reputation. She didn't want word getting around that there was a being in the area more powerful than she was, one who could steal her girls at will. I was also beginning to suspect Helga had agreed to talk to us in the hopes a pair of magic-users might be able to do something where she had failed.

"It sounds like you injured this monster," I said.

"Yes, the being you seek will be half blind. My spell struck its right eye."

That was something, anyway. But we needed a more solid lead. "Do you happen to know if Dawn received a gift of jewelry before her disappearance?" I asked. "A gold bracelet, maybe?"

"Our clients sometimes give them gifts. I do not know about any bracelets."

"Is there someone we could talk to who might?" We needed to milk as much out of the bargain as we could. Lord knew, she would do the same with James when it came task time.

Helga sighed. "You may talk to Carla. She is a friend of Dawn's. You will find her in Lot C."

I bowed. "Thank you, great Matron."

But now that the witch had revealed her weakness, she was not so pleased with the praise. If anything, it seemed to irritate her. Her eyes shifted to James.

"When the time comes to fulfill the bargain, I will send Bolwig. Do not try to back out, or the Eye of Baba will find you. Now leave, both of you." She waved a hand dismissively. "And take your filthy shoes."

Lot C was a triangular expanse of asphalt and chain-link fencing lodged in the northwest corner of the highway exchange. Though it was late morning, massive rigs filled the lot. Several more cruised for empty spaces, diesel engines downshifting, brakes hissing.

Carla, the contact Helga had given us, was in the middle of a job, a girl told us. She'd waved absently in the direction of some parked rigs, and we now sat in James's Jeep facing them, waiting for Carla to emerge.

"Dude, that was intense," James said, twirling his wand around a finger and thumb. I was examining my cane to make sure it hadn't suffered any damage. At Helga's order, the imps had returned our items—by throwing them down into the hotel parking lot. I hoped I'd never have to deal with Helga or her imps again.

"I can't believe you made a bargain with a witch," I said.

"It worked, didn't it?"

"There's a reason I ask you not to talk in those situations. You have no idea what she's going to have you do."

"My problem, not yours."

I gave him a wry look. "Like with the werewolves?"

"Hey, I'll cross those bridges when I get there. It's called taking it one day at a time. You should try it. Might do something for that permanent worry line in your forehead."

"Well, one of your bridges has been pushed back, anyway," I said, letting the dig pass. "Doesn't sound like we're dealing with werewolves."

"I picked up on that too. Any idea who the blond-snatcher could be?"

I set my cane between my legs and shook my head. "Just some vague hunches. The ability to resist Helga's magic suggests either a powerful warlock or something from another plane." We weren't dealing with anything virtuous or protected by a mother's love, that was for damn sure.

"Like a demon?"

"Maybe, but let's not get ahead of ourselves. We need more info. Hopefully, this Carla can provide it."

"Aren't you forgetting something?"

I looked over at James. "Like what?"

"The sheriff's whole song and dance about checking in? Not glancing at a suspect or witness without her say-so?"

"Oh, so now you're a rule hound?"

"Hey, witches and werewolves are one thing, but Marge is another beast altogether. You do not want to get on her sore side. Believe me."

After seeing Marge in action last night, I understood where James was coming from. "Here's the thing," I said, working out the logic as I spoke. "Helga gave *us* permission to talk to Carla, but she didn't say anything about the sheriff's department. They weren't part of the bargain. We let Marge in on this, and she'll want to interview Carla herself. Helga might consider that an affront to her authority and reinstitute the gag order. And then we'll be looking at a big fat goose egg. And *you'll* still be on the hook for the task. We're actually doing Marge a favor here."

"Whatever you have to tell yourself, man," James said. "But when the shit hits the fan, it's your butt, not mine."

"There she is," I said, nodding across the lot. A young woman fitting Carla's description was climbing down from one of the truck cabs. She landed on the asphalt, tottering on her high heels for a moment before straightening her skirt and clacking toward a small concrete bunker house. A red purse dangling from one shoulder slapped her narrow hip.

"C'mon," I said, getting out of the Jeep.

"Shouldn't we let her, you know … clean up first?" James asked. But I was already crossing the lot. I didn't want to lose access to our interviewee. Muttering, James followed at a jog.

We headed Carla off, arriving in front of her. She was older than she'd appeared from a distance. Lines had begun to pinch her eyes, and her exposed belly was going doughy. But Helga's enchantment had a beer-goggling effect. I only realized I was staring when she cocked an eyebrow.

"Help you boys?" Her voice was southern and seductive. *The enchantment*, I reminded myself. I incanted softly to blunt its effect. When Carla spoke again, the same voice sounded croaky. "We don't do two-fers here. One of you's gonna have to wait your turn. I'll let you figure that out. Which rig is yours?" She brought a hand to her brow and squinted around the lot.

"No, no," I said, finding my voice. "We're not here for that."

"Then you best scoot. Our matron doesn't care for gawkers."

"She actually gave us permission to talk to you," I said. "We'd like to ask you some questions about your friend Dawn."

Carla's face stiffened, then turned somber. She leaned her back against the chain-link fence. Only after she'd fished a cigarette from her purse and lit it did she brush the thin, copper-brown hair from her eyes and look up at us again. "What do you wanna know about her?"

"What happened to her?" James blundered in.

When I glared at him, he turned up a hand as though to say, *What?*

"Let's back up," I said to Carla. "First, how well did you know her?"

"I was Dawn's mother." When she saw our confused looks, she explained, "Our matron assigns the new girls a lot-mother, someone to show them the ropes, look out for them, you know. I loved Dawn right off. Little sweetheart, and she learned quick. Didn't need a lot of hand-holding, like most of the newbies 'round here. On our down time, we'd share a smoke and just talk about whatever."

"Did she ever talk about leaving?" I asked.

"If she did, it wasn't to me. Fact, one of the last time's we chatted, she told me she was saving for a down payment on an apartment. Had a place picked out and everything. She figured she'd have enough in 'bout four more months. Was sick of living in the trailer park."

Had someone known that and enticed her with promises of money? I wondered. I thought about the gifts of jewelry some of the other girls had received. "Did Dawn have a significant other?"

Carla snorted smoke from her nose. "Kinda hard to hold onto a man in this line of work, doncha think? Doesn't mean we don't try, but it almost never works out."

"How about an admirer, then?"

"Truckers fall in love with us all the time."

"Can't say I blame them," James put in, flashing his most charming smile. I could see by his eyes that he hadn't bothered to blunt the enchantment. Carla gave him a thorough up and down and smiled back.

I angled myself between them. "Did any of them give Dawn a piece of gold jewelry? It would have been in the days or weeks before her disappearance."

Carla frowned and shook her head. "Not that I can remember." She paused. "Well, now hold on a sec. Last time I saw her, she had on this bracelet. Dull-looking thing, sorta ugly. Not the kind someone would wrap up and tie a bow around. But now that you mention it, the bracelet looked like it coulda been gold."

"Would you mind drawing what it looked like?"

Carla shrugged, parked the cigarette in a corner of her

mouth, and accepted my notepad and pen. A minute later, she handed them back. The sketch, which was surprisingly good, showed a wrist with a thick band encircling it.

"What's this?" I asked, pointing to the top of the bracelet where she'd drawn something that looked like a pi symbol.

"It was scratched in the metal," she said.

A sigil? I wondered. "Did Dawn say where the bracelet came from?"

"No, we didn't talk much that day. She was acting sorta distant, like she was on something."

"Distant how?" I pressed.

"Glassy-eyed. You'd say something, and she'd say 'What?' and you'd have to repeat it. That sort of thing. Our matron wants us to stay clean, for business, you know? She gives any girl who falls off the wagon this gawd-awful drink that cleans them right out, kills the addiction. I was gonna ask Dawn if she needed to go see Helga, but Dawn had already gone home."

"And that was the last time you saw her?" I asked.

Carla nodded and looked off to her left, wiping a tear away with the heel of her palm.

"Guess she got taken like the rest of those girls, huh?"

"That's what we're trying to find out," I said softly. "Did you ever notice anyone watching her? Taking a special interest in her? Not a trucker, necessarily, just anyone who seemed ... different." I was thinking about the symbol and the perp's ability to resist Helga's magic.

"Hey!" someone shouted. "You g-g-get away from her!"

I turned to find a hunched man in blue coveralls shambling toward us, a set of keys jangling from his waist. He looked to be in his forties. A graying bowl cut flopped around his head. He'd been picking up trash with a long grabber, and now he wielded it like a weapon.

"You've g-g-got no business here!" he stuttered.

"Relax, Elmer," Carla called. "They're not hurting me." Then to us in a lowered voice, "Elmer does odd jobs around the lot. A little simple, but he's got a heart of gold. Always been real protective of us girls, even more so since Dawn disappeared."

Elmer arrived in front of us, his bottom lip curling from a set of crooked teeth. He panted as he looked from me to James, his grabber still raised as if he meant to whack one of us in the head. I backed up a half step to make James the easier target.

"Elmer," Carla scolded gently. "Put that down."

Elmer continued to snarl at us, his right eye bloodshot and weeping. "Not g-gonna let them hurt Carla," he said, wiping his eye with a shoulder.

Carla sighed. "It's nothing like that. These men are here to help." She moved behind Elmer and, sliding her hands down his arms, got him to lower the grabber. "There you go, sweetie."

"Yeah, Elmer. We're cool." James raised a hand to high-five him.

When Elmer left him hanging, James clapped him on the shoulder, which made Elmer snarl anew. I used the opportunity to scan him. I didn't pick up any magic, but I still didn't care for his bloodshot eye, not after what Helga had told us: *The being you seek will be half blind.*

"Don't like strange m-men," he said.

"Don't you worry about them," Carla said, pointing past him. "Look, Elmer, your sister's here. Must be lunch time."

A white sports car pulled up, and a woman leaned over to

unlock the passenger side door. Elmer seemed to forget about us as he handed Carla his grabber and plastic garbage bag.

"P-put back?" he asked.

"I'll take care of them," she assured him.

The driver, a bombshell with designer sunglasses and highlights in her blond hair, waved to Carla as Elmer climbed into the passenger seat. "Can I bring you back anything from Micky D's?" she asked.

Carla shook her head. "Naw, I'll grab something from the snack machine later."

"That's a lot of silicone for Grimstone," James whispered, his gaze fixed on Elmer's sister. "But damn, she wears it well."

"Say that a little louder," I muttered. "I don't think her brother heard you."

Elmer's sister waited for Elmer to buckle himself in before pulling away. Elmer squinted menacingly at me and James until the car disappeared behind a line of idling rigs.

"How long has his eye been like that?" I asked Carla.

"Few months? Poked it while using the push broom."

"Must've been a helluva poke," James remarked.

"Well, if that's all the questions you've got..." Carla dropped her cigarette stub on the ground, crushed it out with her heel, and assumed her work face. "My boyfriends are waiting."

"How long has Elmer worked here?" I asked.

"Five years, and you're barking up the wrong tree," she replied as she sashayed toward the concrete bunker that must have served as the girls' personal area. "That man couldn't hurt a fly."

"What now?" James asked me.

"Let's check in with the sheriff."

6

Law enforcement budgets were hurting across the country, and the sight of Grimstone's tiny sheriff's building, a single squad car in the lot, helped me appreciate the tough job Marge had taken on. It also explained why she had little choice but to allow the trucking district to police itself.

When we entered the brown building, a dispatcher pointed James and me to a small office. We found Marge in her sheriff tans at a crowded desk, phone pinned between ear and shoulder.

"I don't care if you've got cancer from your eyeballs to your asshole. If you're not here in ten, you can turn in your badge." She hung up and waved for us to enter. "One of my deputies trying to call out with a sore throat," she explained. "Told him that's what lozenges are for."

"Good point," I said meekly, taking a seat. James wedged into the chair beside me. Both our knees touched the front of her desk.

She consulted the notes in front of her. "I checked, and

you were onto something, Croft. The vics are all natural blondes." I nodded at the news, not surprised. "So, what do you have for *me*?" she asked.

"We spoke to Helga this morning, and we learned a few things," I answered quickly. I'd warned James on the drive over not to say anything about our conversation with Carla, but given that my warnings thus far had fallen on deaf ears, I was determined to beat him to every response.

"She talked to you?" Marge asked.

"It, ah, took a little negotiating, but yeah. The night Dawn disappeared, Helga used an enchanted object to look for her. But whoever or whatever took Dawn attacked Helga through the object. From the way Helga told it, she barely survived. She gouged her attacker's eye to get away."

"Did she get a look at her assailant?"

"No, but she says whoever it was will have a wounded right eye."

"Does she have any idea how the perp made off with Dawn?"

"Well, Dawn was seen wearing a gold bracelet a few days before she disappeared. Given what the boyfriends of those other two girls said, it sounds like that's how the perp is making first contact with them. The bracelet was old and dull. And there was a design on the top of it." I opened my notepad and turned it around so Marge could see Carla's drawing.

She squinted at it. "Haven't seen that before. Know what it means?"

"Not specifically, but we might be looking at a ritual. The victims are in their early twenties, an age of fecundity. And blond hair carries a specific charge, sometimes used in magic. Add to that the fact they're disappearing on the full moon, a time of power, and yeah … More than enticing the victims, the jewelry could be enthralling them, getting them to cooperate in the ritual." I thought about Dawn's distractedness the night before she'd disappeared.

"What kind of ritual?"

"I hate to say it, but probably the sacrificial kind."

Marge nodded grimly. "Go on."

"Ritual sacrifice is as old as civilization," I said, slipping into professor mode. "The ancient Canaanites sacrificed infants to the god Moloch. China's second oldest dynasty dismembered prisoners of war, offering the parts to Shang-Di, 'lord from above.' There are scores of other examples, but in almost every case, the ritual sacrifices are used to curry favor with a god—"

"Or demon," James interrupted.

"Thank you, I was getting to that. *Or demon*, with the hope of some gain. That explains not only the power Helga felt, but the overwhelming sense of greed."

"What does the perp want?" Marge asked.

"Depends on who it is," I answered. "If we're talking about a warlock or sorcerer, maybe nothing more complicated than power."

"And how would we stop someone like that?"

"First we have to find them." Though I'd sensed no magic around the janitor who had accosted us in Lot C, I kept seeing his red, weeping eye. "Do you happen to know a guy with a hunched back named Elmer? Does odd jobs around the trucking lots?"

"Elmer Fratelli. What about him?"

"He seems to have a strange relationship with the girls working the lot. Protective of them, but overly so. He would have known Dawn, and—"

"'We begin by coveting what we see every day'?" Marge interrupted with an eye roll. "*Silence of the Lambs* wins Best Picture, and suddenly everyone's an FBI profiler," she muttered.

"Well, she *was* the first victim," I pointed out. "And Elmer has an injury to his right eye."

But like Carla, Marge dismissed the idea. "Elmer doesn't have it here or here to sacrifice anyone," she said, tapping her temple and heart. "And he's never been in any trouble. Only time we ever had a call to his place was because he'd walked out of the house and forgotten to pull on some pants. He's got a sister who looks after him. She's a social worker, so he has the services he needs. If he's not working at the lot, he's at home being looked after."

"Doesn't sound like our man, then," I said, though without complete conviction.

She narrowed her salty blue eyes at me. "What were you doing in the lot to begin with?"

Damn. In my peripheral vision, I could see James leaning away from me. "A reading," I lied.

"A reading of what?" she demanded.

"Just a general, you know ... reading." I swallowed dryly. "The lot was Dawn's last known whereabouts, so I wanted to see if I could pick up anything that might be useful. Energies, auras, that sort of thing."

"Sounds like a load of horseshit," Marge said. "You talked to one of the girls, didn't you? That's how you came face to face with Elmer. Or more likely, how he came face to face with you."

Rather than dig my hole any deeper, I mumbled, "Something like that."

"What did I tell you last night?"

"That we weren't to do anything investigation-wise without your say-so." I felt like I was back in the grade school principal's office.

"And here I thought *you* were going to be the responsible one."

The guilt at having disappointed her pulled on my gut. "It's just that Helga gave us permission, and I was afraid that if we brought the sheriff's department back in, she'd rescind the offer—or worse. It wasn't my intention to subvert your authority. Honestly."

But Marge wasn't in the mood for an explanation. Planting her hands on her desk, she leaned toward me until I could see the tiny veins on her nose. "You check in with me from now on. Got it, mister?"

"Yes, ma'am," I said.

"If I have to tell you again, I'll run you out of Grimstone myself." I had no doubt she would. Her eyes cut back and forth over mine for several tense beats. At last, she pushed herself from her desk and limped around it and out the door. "You two coming?" she called back.

James elbowed me in the side as we stood.

"Told you so," he whispered.

"Shut it," I whispered back.

We followed Marge into an adjoining file room. Stacks of boxes lined the floor and sat on metal shelves. "You asked for some of the victims' belongings," she said, directing our attention to a small table. "Will these do?"

I looked over the items she'd laid out: a smartphone, a fork, a purple scrunchie, and what looked like a folded-up note.

"These are actually really good. This one in particular," I said, indicating the scrunchie. A few blond strands of hair had gotten snagged in the elastic. "Should hold a lot of essence."

"Well, don't let me stop you. I'll be in my office if you need anything."

As she limped back out, closing the door behind her, James regarded the items dubiously. "Are you really thinking of casting a hunting spell after what happened to the witch?"

It was something I'd been worrying about, too. If the perp could get to Helga through the Eye of Baba, they could almost certainly get to me through a hunting spell. But for a solid lead, we needed the location of the disappeared girls. "Ever heard of a Hadrian Circle?" I asked him.

"You're gonna summon this thing?"

If we were more powerful, that might have been an option—calling up the god or demon, compelling it to tell us who it was working for, and then banishing it. But we weren't that powerful.

"That's how Hadrian Circles are most often used, yes, as a container for a summoned being. But I've also read of practitioners reversing the circle's polarity and turning it into a powerful protective barrier. It takes considerably less energy to bar something than to contain it."

But my partner continued to look at the girls' personal items warily. "Witches and werewolves are one thing," he said. "I can see and touch and shoot them, you know? I'm even cool with shallow demons. But these things coming up from deeper down... I don't know, man."

"Does this have anything to do with your possession as a kid?"

When James was thirteen, a demon had attached itself to him, no doubt attracted to his latent power. Through him, the demon had performed several heinous acts before being banished by a member of the Order.

"Probably," James admitted.

"I get it, man. I've been there too. Hell, my demon's still with me." I was referring to Thelonious, a boozing, womanizing incubus with whom I'd struck a deal back in grad school. Since then, I'd developed enough capacity to keep him away. Not so much when my powers were depleted, though.

"Yeah, but yours is a partier," James said. "This one sounds like a total freak."

"I'll be the one casting the hunting spell. I'll just need your help to reverse and sustain the circle, to protect me long enough to establish a connection to the girl. Shouldn't take more than a minute."

"And then you're out?"

"And then I'm out," I assured him.

James chewed on that for a minute.

"It's nice to see this more prudent side of you, by the way." He nodded and sighed. "All right. Let's do this."

I cleared the table of everything but the scrunchie. I then pulled a tall vial of copper filings from my pocket and sprinkled a basic casting circle around the item with its snagged strands of hair. The Hadrian Circle took more time to build, a pattern of concentric rings and sigils that encircled the entire table.

When I finished, I grasped my cane and stepped inside the circle's outer ring.

"Okay, here's how this is going to go. I'll activate the Hadrian Circle. Once it's up, I want you to imbue this sigil here." I pointed at the symbol that protruded from the circle like a single atom from a molecular diagram. "That will reverse the polarity. You'll then need to sustain it. It's going to take a good deal of power, but I'll work as fast as I can. No matter what happens, keep your focus on the sigil."

James nodded and pulled his wand from his vest pocket. He still looked uneasy.

"We've got this," I said, nudging him with my cane.

"Hope so, man."

Training my focus on the circle around my feet, I said, *"Cerrare."*

The pressure in my ears changed as the circle snapped closed. I opened my mental prism, allowing energy to course through me and into the circle. The curving lines and symbols began to glow. Outside, James's image warped and wavered as a column of air hardened around the table and me.

I tapped the column with the end of my cane to tell him it was time.

He aimed his wand at the sigil and, lips moving, released a stream of silver light. It took a minute for the sigil to activate, but when it did, it felt like a switch being thrown. The pressure that had enclosed me in silence underwent an inversion, filling my ears with a sudden roaring.

I took a moment to assess the Hadrian Circle—it felt potent, like a living force—before moving my cane over the scrunchie on the tabletop. My mouth moved with an incantation. White light swelled from the opal in my cane, inhaling the threads of smoke drifting up from the hairs.

Now to connect to the target.

I peeked over at James. He was maintaining the sigil, but the silver light revealed a sheen of sweat over his trembling face. I would have to hurry. I incanted the Words, and seconds later, my cane jiggled.

"I have her," I called to James, giving him a thumb's up.

The most dangerous phase of a hunting spell was establishing the connection. That initial burst of energy had made me highly visible—and thus highly vulnerable. But now that I had the connection, I was safe again. It was just a matter now of following the thread to its—

I choked as a violent force crunched my throat closed.

Outside the circle, James's lips were moving: *Hey, man, you all right?*

I dropped my cane and collapsed to my knees.

Prof! he shouted. *What's going on?*

My partner's face clenched as more silver energy poured from his wand and into the sigil, but it was no good. Whatever had me was past the defenses, strangling off my air. I moved my hands to my throat, but I couldn't feel anything. The attack was coming from another plane.

Tell me what to do, dammit! James shouted.

Can't exactly breathe here, pal, I thought desperately.

I pawed for my cane, which had landed beside me. But as my fingers closed around the shaft, darkness closed over my vision, and I was no longer in the sheriff's department.

7

One of my hands continued to paw at my throat, but I'd stopped choking. Lowering the arm slowly, I turned in a circle. The space around me was pitch black. When I inhaled, I smelled the stink of death.

"James?" I called.

The fading echoes warped my partner's name until it sounded like something alien. *Need some light.* I patted my chest, but my coin pendant was gone. Neither was my cane in hand. With nothing to cast through, I began feeling my way forward. I needed to find a way out of here.

Wherever *here* was.

I thought back to my attempt to cast on the scrunchie. Something had come through the hunting spell, gotten past the Hadrian Circle, and seized my throat, pulling me into ... a parallel realm?

If you're lucky, I thought with a shaky snort. *You could just as well be dead.*

A cold draft slipped past. I pivoted toward it, hoping it marked an opening back to the sheriff's department. Arms outstretched, I sped my pace. But now I felt something following me.

Wheeling around, I stared into the blackness. Marge had brought up *The Silence of the Lambs* earlier, and I suddenly felt like I was in the scene at the end when Agent Starling was in the killer's basement, the killer tracking her with night-vision goggles.

A low moan sounded.

"Who are you?" I demanded.

The being didn't respond. Or perhaps it did, because in the next moment I felt the greed Helga had described oozing around me like a tide of tar. The stink of death grew stronger, as though something long buried were breaking the surface, filling the air with its decaying gases.

I pushed power into my wizard's voice. "Let me out of here."

The moaning became a single, hungry word: "Soon..."

It took me a moment to realize what the being meant. I might not be choking down here, but back on the physical plane, the force around my throat was still strangling me. My body would be oxygen starved, undergoing slow brain death, fluids seeping into my lungs...

Hot panic broke through me. *"Respingere!"* I cried.

I threw my mental prism open, but the invocation that typically resulted in an explosive release of power only let off the reserve already inside me, which wasn't much. It was like attempting to throw a punch in water. The being didn't react to the feeble manifestation.

Think, Everson. Think, dammit.

Madam Helga had repelled the being, but she had been anchored in her world, with local power to cast from. I was in a plane devoid of ley energy. My mind grasped for alternate currents of power.

Right now, a thread of energy was running from my cane to one of the missing girls. If she had been sacrificed, then the thread would connect the cane to the being, explaining how it had attacked me. I may not have had my cane, but I could access that thread.

Still need a power source, though... The Hadrian Circle! I thought suddenly.

It operated on multiple planes. If James was still sustaining the circle, I could attempt to tap into it, use it to drive an attack into the being.

Closing my eyes, I first felt for the connection between the cane and the being. I found it, a slender vibrating thread, and took it in an astral hand. Stretching out my other arm, I felt for the energy of the Hadrian Circle.

C'mon, James, please tell me you're still pushing power through it.

It was a long shot. Despite what I'd told him, he'd probably come over to help me. I imagined him kneeling beside me as my face purpled, cycling through every invocation he knew to get the being to release my throat, the circle pulsing dimmer and dimmer as it expired.

But then I felt a familiar pattern of energy.

Oh, bless you, child, I thought toward James.

I seized the potent energy, drew in a breath, and shouted, *"Disfare!"*

Raw energy released from the circle. I called in as much as I could, channeling it through the hunting spell. The thread swelled as power went storming down its length and into the being.

I drew a savage breath and sat bolt upright. Fluorescent lights seared my eyes as my lids peeled back and my chest grabbed a lungful of oxygen. My throat felt raw and swollen, and I could taste blood.

"Shit, man, what happened?" James asked.

He dropped into a crouch beside me, the tip of his wand dimming. All around us boxes and files had spilled from their shelves, probably when I yanked the energy into the other realm. Smoke rose from the spent casting circle. I nodded to tell James I was all right, then fell into a fit of coughing.

"How long was I down?" I wheezed.

"I don't know, fifteen, twenty seconds. Scared the crap out of me."

"I got pulled in," I said, pushing myself to my knees.

As James helped me stand, the door opened. I followed Marge's severe gaze around the trashed room. "What in holy hell happened in here?" Our condition seemed the least of her concerns.

"Made contact with one of the girls," I managed, my throat still on fire. "But whatever took them grabbed me. Pulled me into some other realm. Dark place, smelled like death. I had to blow the connection to the girl to get out of there. Apologies for the mess."

"So, we got nothing out of that," Marge said in summation.

My encounter in the alternate realm *had* given me a better sense of what we might be dealing with, but I knew what Marge meant. We didn't have a thread to the missing girls anymore. Because, God knew, I wasn't going to attempt a hunting spell on the remaining items.

"We've got less than a day until the snatcher strikes again," Marge reminded us. "Some poor girl is probably already walking around with a gold bracelet, no idea she's next on the list."

Yeah, I thought, *and the longer the being has access to our world, the larger his portal becomes. All kinds of horrors could squeeze through. If James thinks he's got it bad here now, he's going to love—*

"The bracelet," he said suddenly. Marge and I turned toward him. A light seemed to illuminate his blue eyes. "That's how we can locate the next victim. And once we have the bracelet, we can figure out its origin."

"Nice idea," I said, "but we have no connection to the bracelet."

"I'm not talking about a connection. I'm just talking about the knowledge. I don't know how the perp is getting the bracelet to these girls, but I'm guessing anonymously. Which means the girls could think they have a secret admirer, right? Well, what if we riffed on that."

"*Riffed* on that how?" Marge said.

"Flood the local social media sites, take out an ad in the paper, maybe get something on the radio. It could be like a personal ad. You know, 'To the girl of my dreams. I gave you a bracelet. Would you give me a call? Your Secret Admirer.' Something like that. Word would have to get to her eventually, right? Seems a solid fifty-fifty that her curiosity would get the better of her and she'd pick up the phone."

I stared at James. "That's actually a good idea."

"For a change," Marge added.

We gathered back in her office where Marge and James began drafting the ad. While they worked, I touched the end of my cane to my throat and spoke healing incantations.

"I know the editor at the *Star*," Marge said. "I'll get him to run this for the next few days. And we have an agreement with the local radio station for announcements. I'll have Deputy Franks post on the forums." She checked her watch and muttered, "If he ever gets his ass in here."

At that moment, the front door to the building banged opened.

"Speak of the devil," Marge muttered.

"Hey, Sheriff," the deputy called in a voice that sounded like it was still in the throes of puberty. But when James and I turned, we were looking at a lanky man with thinning hair. He didn't so much walk as stumble toward us, his highway-patrolman sunglasses jostling between a pair of large ears. I could tell he thought the glasses made him look tough.

"Deputy, this is Everson Croft," Marge said as I lowered my cane and extended a hand. "He's teaming up with Wesson to help us with the disappearance cases."

Franks's hand was damp when we shook. "You a magician too?" he asked.

"Not quite," I answered thinly, my voice mostly healed from the strangling. The deputy's voice, on the other hand, sounded a little hoarse. Bluish shadows stood in the pits of his bony cheeks.

Marge wrinkled her nose. "Have you been drinking?"

I picked up the strong scent too, a mixture of turpentine and pure alcohol.

"Oh, that." Franks smacked his lips, and his Adam's apple bulged when he swallowed. "I know you suggested lozenges, but there's this old remedy my grandmother swore by. Supposed to cure any ailment."

"Good, because we've got work for you." She gestured to the notepad on her desk. "Got some ads I want you to post.

We'll station you on the department's backup line to field responses."

"What then?" I asked.

"Well, if a girl calls and can accurately describe the bracelet, we'll pick her up and put her in protective custody."

"I'm not sure that's a good idea," I said.

Marge's brow folded downward. I got the impression she wasn't used to being contradicted.

"Look," I said, "we don't know what kind of control the bracelet exerts over the girls. If the perp knows she's been picked up, he or she could compel the wearer to harm herself—or the ones protecting her. And it might not be so easy to pull the bracelet off her, either. I'm betting it's going to require magic to safely remove. I think our approach has to be more subtle."

"More subtle how?" Marge asked.

"Getting her to agree to meet out," I said.

"Out? Like on a date?"

"I guess you could call it that."

"And no disrespect to the deputy here," James cut in, "but I think Everson and I should handle that part of things."

Marge looked over at Franks, who was thrusting his neck forward like a chicken as he tried to clear his throat. "You've got a point," she said. "But what's to stop the thing from attacking you again?"

"The one advantage of having been dragged into its world is that I have a better idea of what we're dealing with," I said. "First, I didn't get a demon vibe. I got much more of a ... death vibe. The smell of the place, the way the being talked. Like I was in the underworld of a pagan god. Some of them are resistant to magic, which would explain how it penetrated our protective circle. We find out *which* god, and we can very likely destroy it."

"And how are you going to find that out?" Marge asked.

"Research. I have a suitcase full of books back at James's place. But first I want to stop at the local library, see if there's anything in the archives that matches the pattern of disappearances."

"We have all that stuff databased," Marge said. "Didn't find diddly."

"I'm talking *way* back. Like, to the founding of Grimstone."

"Knock yourself out," she said. "Okay, we'll use your number for the ad, Wesson." She narrowed her eyes at my partner before shifting them back to me. "But if the girl *does* call, the department is going to be involved in anything you arrange. Are we clear?"

"Yes, ma'am," James and I answered in unison.

8

James drummed his fingers against the steering wheel as he drove us across town. The beats became more and more emphatic, to the point I couldn't think.

"Do you mind?" I snapped.

"Oh, sorry." He stopped drumming and gripped the wheel. "Just getting excited."

"For a library visit? I didn't realize the prospect of research did that for you."

"Naw," he chuckled. "I've got my eye on this chick who works there."

"Well, I'm going to need both of your eyes on the newspaper archives."

"She wears reading glasses and these conservative sweaters," he went on, his smile growing broader. "But the way she wears them. Whoa, momma." He shook his head and propped his forearm on the windowsill. "I'm telling you, there's a she-tiger crouching inside. Just wait till you see her, man."

"Can't wait," I muttered.

"She mostly blows me off, but I'm playing the long game with this one. The end's a foregone conclusion, though. Always is," he said with a cocky grin. "Her name's Myrtle."

"Myrtle?" I pictured an old woman with a dowager's hump and orthopedic shoes.

"Don't let the name fool you, bro. She is fine with a capital F."

"I'll take your word for it, but look, we've got a lot of material to go through and not a lot of time. Focus, man. I'm serious. Your idea about the ad was brilliant. I need more of that from you."

"It *was* pretty brilliant, wasn't it?"

"But it's only one iron," I added quickly. "We need to get as many in the fire as we can."

I was new to this whole mentoring thing. I didn't want to lean on James so hard that he turned resentful, but neither did I want to inflate his already considerable ego. There was a balance in there somewhere.

"All right, Prof. Point taken."

James straightened and turned the Jeep onto Main Street. Grimstone's north-south drag had a distinctively western look. Along the flat-fronted blocks, restaurants stood beside antique furniture stores and coffee shops. Families in colorful attire ambled the sidewalks. "Only part of town that's actually nice," James remarked. "The highways bring in a few tourists."

A short, squat man in an antiquated suit and pie hat caught my eye. He was waddling up and down the sidewalk, trying to get passers-by to step into a real estate office located beside a mining museum. Through my open window, I caught barked phrases like "Once in a lifetime opportunity!"

and "Don't miss it!" Trim the swaying orange beard and the man could have been a carnival barker.

"Who's he?" I asked, nodding.

"Oh, that's Tjalf," James answered with a snort. "Everyone in town calls him Taffy. Member of the Brunhold clan. One of the sons, I think. Or maybe a grandson. I can't keep them all straight. He's one of the few with personality, though."

"They're the developers, right?" I asked, remembering what Marge had said at James's house the night before.

"And dwarves."

"Dwarves? You mean actual dwarves, not just the short-in-stature kind?"

"The real deal," James said. "They settled in the area a long time ago. Used their dwarf know-how to mine out the precious metals, then plowed their wealth into development and real estate. Have a monopoly in Grimstone County. They all live in a compound together. Kind of strange."

I repeated the name. "Tjalf Brunhold. That's old German."

"I know that look, Prof. Your brain's chewing on something."

"Well, a lot of pagan gods come from that region of Europe. And with dwarves capable of harnessing powerful magic..."

"You think they could be summoning the god?"

"I think they're worth keeping in mind. That's all."

When the dwarf spun toward us, I was too slow to look away. I waited a second, then snuck another peek. Sudden anger seized his face as his animated eyes turned the color of stone. Naturally, the light at the intersection chose that moment to cycle to red, and we rolled to a stop right beside him. I averted my gaze, pretending to become interested in the street sign.

"See something green?" Taffy barked. When I didn't answer, he waddled up to the Jeep and kicked it. The impact was violent, shaking the vehicle. I'd read about dwarf strength, but damn. "Hey, pencil neck, I'm talking to you."

"Oh," I said, pretending to notice him for the first time. "Is there a problem down there?"

I was resorting to wise-assery—probably not the best example for James—but I hadn't cared for the dwarf's characterization of me. Taffy's cheeks hardened into red garnets. "How about I beat you into the sidewalk so you can see for yourself if there's a problem *down here?*"

He tried to open my door, which I'd fortunately locked. His hands shot up and groped for me through the open window.

"What the...?"

I leaned back and slapped at his hairy fingers. The dwarf huffed and grunted as he jumped up to reach me. On his third attempt, he managed to grasp the shoulder of my coat and pull me against the door. As I fought to free myself, I imagined his stubby feet kicking above the street.

"Wait!" James called, trying his hardest not to laugh. "Hey, it's cool, man, it's cool."

The dwarf stopped trying to extract me through the window and took a few steps back. He squinted as he fixed his pie hat. Short-sightedness was another one of their traits.

"James?" he asked, still squinting. They were also too proud to wear glasses.

"Yeah, it's me. Everson here's a friend of mine from out of town. I'm just showing him around."

"Well, you need to tell your friend that this isn't a freak show."

"No worries, man," he said. "I'll tell him. You doing all right?"

"Business as usual," he grunted, straightening his jacket.

"I'll stop in one of these days, see what's on the market. Might be looking for a place soon." The light changed. "All right, Taffy. Hang loose, bro."

"It's Tjalf!" he shouted as we rolled away.

James laughed and punched me in the arm. "Told you he had personality."

"Just a little," I muttered, my heart still slamming. I smoothed out the wadded-up ball of fabric where Taffy had grabbed my coat, watching his diminishing figure through the side mirror. He was back to hailing passers-by—"The best investment money can buy!"—but our encounter was a good reminder that no matter how they looked or talked, dwarves were not to be messed with.

Especially true if they had a pagan god on their side.

A minute later, James turned off Main Street and into a small lot. A two-story building of gray stone rose in front of us: the Grimstone County Library. Though small, it exuded a dignified air. Something told me I was going to be right at home inside.

"Damn, she's not here today," James said.

"Myrtle? How do you know?"

"Her car's not in the lot."

"Bummer," I said.

We entered the library and spoke with the librarian on duty, an elderly woman who looked like a Myrtle but whose nametag read "Britney." She led us through the stacks to a room where a giant set of beige drawers held microfilm of the town paper going back to its first edition. Britney wanted to stay and show us how to use the directory and microfilm viewers, but we assured her we were fine. She left looking disappointed.

"So how should we do this?" James asked, taking a seat in front of the directory.

"Let's start with a keyword search. 'Disappearance,' 'Abduction,' 'Murder,' 'Serial.' Put them in one at a time."

James complied. "Getting a ton of hits."

"Let's narrow it down, then. Marge said nothing came up in her database, so let's go back to pre-1980."

James tapped the keyboard and nodded. "Better."

"Print off the results, and then do the same for the remaining keywords. We'll split the list and each take a microfilm machine."

"I was so hoping Myrtle would be here," he said wistfully.

"James. Focus."

Four hours later, I scrolled to the final article on my list—an attempted murder in September 1884. I scanned the story with straining eyes, but it was about a saloon owner firing at a man she claimed owed a gambling debt. I peered over at James. The more things changed...

"Anything?" I asked him.

For the past hour James had been sighing and grumbling, obviously tiring of the search. But now he was leaning toward the viewer, his illuminated face absorbed in whatever he was reading.

"Maybe..." he answered faintly.

I stood and came up behind him.

"Two broads disappeared in the early 1900s, but they caught the dude. Rancher named Sten Klausen."

"Blond?" I asked, squinting to read the grainy text.

"No mention of his hair color."

"Not him, dummy. The women."

"Relax, Prof, I'm just messing with you. Doesn't say. One was a nurse and the other a visiting teacher." His lips moved quietly as he read. "And look! They disappeared a month apart."

I caught up to where he was in the article and jotted down the dates: exactly thirty days apart. If we were looking at full moons, we definitely had something. James and I read the rest of the story in silence. Sten was arrested on suspicion after making a drunken boast in a saloon that not only would the missing women never be recovered but that there would be more disappearances.

As of the writing of the article, the women hadn't been found.

"Sten Klausen," I muttered, writing down the name. "Let's do a search on this guy. See what we can find."

"Way ahead of you, Prof," James said, already wheeling toward the computer.

"Sten died in jail a month after his capture," someone said.

I turned to find a young woman wearing reading glasses and a gray cardigan standing in the doorway. She was rigid in a scholarly way, her brunette bun wound so tight it pulled up the skin of her brow. It took me a moment to realize I was looking at James's crush. She adjusted the stack of books in her arms.

"Asphyxiation," she added.

"Myr—Myrtle," James stammered. "I didn't realize you were working today."

She ignored him and turned to resume shelving her books.

"Wait," I called, hurrying to catch up. "How do you know that?"

"It's my job to know. I'm on the board of the Grimstone County Historical Society."

"Do you mind if I ask you a few questions, then?"

"And you are...?"

"Everson Croft. I'm working with James here."

James removed his cowboy hat and ran a hand over his hair. Instead of acknowledging him, Myrtle walked her fingers down a row of call numbers and slotted a book home. "What do you want to know?"

"Do you happen to know whether the victims had blond hair?"

She hesitated for a moment, head tilted. "As a matter of fact, they did."

James and I exchanged a knowing look. "What else can you tell us about Sten Klausen?" I asked.

"He emigrated with his wife from Denmark. They first settled in Kansas before moving to Grimstone County. They homesteaded on two hundred acres. Sten bought more than four hundred head of steer, but his first winter here was brutal. Lost all but a few dozen. He had to go back to the bank for a loan to replace them. The next winter didn't go much better, but the bank refused him a third loan. He had a mining claim, but the Great Quake of 1902 probably took care of that. There was speculation the situation drove him to drink. His wife left him and moved back to Kansas. With no marriage prospects, Sten must have become desperate. Probably what led him to abduct those women."

James gave an impressed chuckle. "That's a lot of info. Do you have a photographic memory? If so, I'd love to test it. Maybe over dinner one of these nights?"

I shook my head to tell him now wasn't the time. If Sten had indeed invoked the underworld god I'd encountered, we needed to figure out why. And how. Calling up a pagan god usually required a relic of some kind. One that might have ended up in the hands of an heir.

"Did he have any children?" I asked Myrtle.

"Two sons and a daughter," she said. "One of the sons died in childhood, and his wife took the remaining two children with her."

I followed her down the aisle. "Did the surviving children inherit the ranch?"

"No, it was repossessed by the bank and auctioned off."

"Are there any records of who purchased it?"

"The auctioning bank was Western Frontier, but they failed in the 1930s during the Depression. Their records changed ownership a few times, but thanks to an acquisition I helped spearhead, the records are in storage at the Historical Society."

"Really?" I said with a little too much excitement.

Myrtle paused long enough in her reshelving to slip me a sidelong smile. I glanced over at James to find him frowning. Wait, was she flirting with me? Maybe there was a feline in there after all.

"Um, is there any way you could check for us?" I asked her. "It would really help."

"I'm heading over to the Society later. I'll take a look." She shelved the final book and produced a pen and square of paper from a clipboard. "Write down your number and I'll give you a call."

In one deft move, James stepped around me and took the pen and paper. "Actually, we're working on this together, so let me go ahead and give you my digits..." When James finished writing, he dangled the paper in front of her and spoke in a teasing voice. "You promise you'll call as soon as you know something?"

Myrtle's brow furrowed. Before she could decide we were a couple of d-bags not worth helping, I snatched the paper from James and handed it to her. "We really appreciate this," I said.

"*Both* of us do," James put in. "And that's my personal number, so if you ever want to, you know—"

He grunted as I elbowed him in the ribs. "Start the search on Sten," I whispered harshly. He grumbled and scuffed back to the microfilm room. Before Myrtle could turn away, I said, "You mentioned Sten asphyxiated in jail. Did he hang himself with a bed sheet or something?"

A conspiratorial look came over Myrtle's face. "That's still as much a question as the women who disappeared. The bailiff locked him up for the night. When he checked on Sten the next morning, the bedding was all over the cell, and Sten was dead. There was bruising around his neck. People assumed a vigilante group had gotten to him—not uncommon in Grimstone County back then—but the bailiff swore up and down no one came that night."

"So, he just ... died," I said, touching my own recently strangled throat.

"I love a good mystery. Anyway, I'll let you know what I find out about the auction."

"I'm especially interested in his personal effects."

Myrtle gave a final coy smile and walked off quietly in her flats. *Good,* I thought, *that gets another iron in the fire.*

I joined James back in the microfilm room. He was consulting a page from the printer while pulling a box of film from a drawer.

"Way to throw a cock-block there, Prof," he said.

"We're supposed to be working, remember? Anyway, she's not interested in you."

"I told you, it's a work in progress."

I stood behind him as he loaded a roll into the viewer. The first hit on Sten was before the disappearances and had to do with the formation of a local cattlemen's association. James centered the viewer on a photo of six men in front of the town livery—officers of the new association dressed in their western best.

My gaze fell to the caption below.

"There," I said, spotting Sten Klausen's name. "Second from the right. Can you zoom in?"

James centered the viewer on Sten, adjusting the focus as he expanded the image. The man growing in front of us had pale, staring eyes, a thin nose, and a light-colored beard that hid his mouth. "What's that he's wearing?" James asked, edging the viewer down slightly. "A star?"

I squinted at the blurry object hanging over Sten's chest. I saw where it could be mistaken for a five-pointed star, but the top point was blunt and rounded. I'd seen one of those before.

"It's a human-shaped idol," I said. "Some of the Norse cults used them to communicate with gods."

9

"So, you think someone's using the same idol?" James asked as he drove us back to his place. He'd taken the top panels off the Jeep, and the afternoon air and sun felt good after the chill of the morning.

"I'm sure of it," I said. "Sten's victims were young women, blond, and I'll look it up as soon as we get inside, but I'm going to go ahead and say they disappeared near full moons. Throw in Sten's death by strangulation…"

"But wouldn't that mean he was a victim too?"

"Yeah, of the god's wrath. Myrtle said he died a month after his incarceration, which would have been the next full moon—when the god was expecting another sacrifice. When Sten didn't deliver, the god paid him a visit."

"Did him like the god tried to do you," James said in understanding. "So which god are we talking about?"

"Based on my encounter, I'm going with a version of Hel, Norse goddess of the underworld." I thought of the pervasive death smell from when I'd been attacked back at the station.

"Why her?"

"I'll consult my books, but if I were to go by the Old Norse literature, I'd say Sten wanted to bring someone back from the dead."

"Like resurrection?"

"In one of the few myths in which Hel is featured, a group of gods pled with her to restore another god to life. They wanted her to do it quickly. If a god remains dead for too long, they lose most of their faculties, become zombie-like. Anyway, after Sten's family left him, he may have tried to bring back his lost son, the one Myrtle said died in childhood."

"Makes sense, but sacrificing blond-haired women on the full moon?"

"It's horrible, but it would have gotten Hel's attention. A similar motive could be driving someone now."

"Son of a bitch," James said.

I began to nod in agreement before realizing he wasn't referring to the sacrifices. I followed his squinting gaze to his distant trailer. Smoke rose from it in a black column. It was on fire.

"Annie," James said, pressing the gas.

The Jeep shook down the dirt drive, bouncing in and out of potholes. We had locked his dog inside when we left. I gripped the overhead bar and aimed my cane at the approaching trailer.

"Cerrare!" I shouted.

White light burst forth, surrounding the fiery building in a glimmering orb. I grunted against the heat as I began to draw the orb down, squeezing out the available oxygen. The flames pushed back. Sweat sprang from my hairline and spilled into my eyes, even with the wind blasting my face. I blinked away the sting while fighting to shrink the orb even further.

At last, the fire died. I held on for several more moments to be sure before releasing the invocation with a gasp.

James slewed to a stop, tires throwing dust over the blackened porch. He leapt from the Jeep and bounded up the porch steps. As he yanked the door open, he shouted an invocation to draw the air from the house. The sudden outpouring of smoke blew his cowboy hat off. He lowered his head and entered, calling his dog's name: "Annie!"

As I approached the trailer, I felt what remained of James's wards crackling around the cement foundation—probably the only thing that had prevented his home from being reduced to a smoldering heap. I circled the house to make sure whoever had set the blaze was now gone.

I returned to the front at the same moment James emerged through the door, his dog limp in his arms. "She's barely breathing," he said desperately, descending the porch steps.

"Set her down here," I told him.

James lay Annie gently on the ground. Her eyes were closed, pink tongue hanging from the side of her mouth. The rise and fall of her torso was shallow and hoarse. Touching my cane to Annie's chest, I began to incant. A gauzy white light grew from the opal end of my cane, enveloping the pit bull. Her body spasmed, and drool ran down her tongue.

"C'mon, girl," James said, kneeling beside her.

I eased back on the healing energy, watching for a response. Moments later, Annie hacked twice, then released a weak whimper. As the gauzy light dissipated, her eyes opened. She blinked up at me, then craned her neck back enough to lick James's knee.

"Thank God," James breathed, rubbing her neck. "You scared me, girl."

Annie licked him some more, then rested her head back down and closed her eyes. She was going to be all right. Crisis averted, I picked up a brass casing beside my shoe and held it up.

"These are all around the trailer," I said, "along with sets of large tire tracks."

James took the 9mm casing and looked it over. "Damned wolves," he muttered, chucking it away. The automatic gunfire had weakened James's already weak wards enough for them to torch the trailer. It could have been worse. Of course, it never had to happen in the first place. I'd be a jerk to point that out, though. My partner had nearly lost his dog.

"I'm almost afraid to ask," I said. "But how's the inside?"

"Not too terrible. Looks like most of the damage is to the exterior."

James ordered Annie to stay as he and I climbed the front steps. I eyed the charred porch and melted siding dubiously, but when we stepped inside, it was actually in fair condition. The fire had only begun to curl under the eaves, streaking parts of the ceiling black. As James struggled to open windows, I expelled the lingering smoke with a force invocation.

"Hopefully, Santana made his point," James said, "and he'll be cool with settling up now."

"Hopefully," I agreed, though with much less confidence than James. The last thing we needed was another confrontation with that bunch. We had a god of the undead to find and destroy.

In the living room, I hefted my suitcase onto the pullout couch and selected several thick tomes. In one, I checked the moon cycles back in 1902 and compared them with the dates in my notepad. Sure enough, the first disappearance had occurred two days before the full moon and the second was on the full moon itself.

Sten's death a month later would have coincided with a third full moon.

I told James this as I stacked the remaining books on his table. He was filling Annie's water dish at the kitchen sink.

"So, what are you looking for now?" he asked.

"A few things. First, any info I can find on the idol and bracelet. Second, how to protect us from Hel, should she attack again. And third, how to banish her back to her realm for good."

"Can we do that?" James asked. "I mean, she sounds like a pretty major god."

"She is and she isn't. Mythology uses one name for gods like Hel, but there are actually many variations of them, depending on the cult that worships them. The collective belief in a god creates the template. Specific rites performed over time shape the gods into individual beings."

"And you're saying there's one version of Hel that has a taste for young blondes on the full moon."

"Exactly."

"How do you figure out which one that is, though?"

"That's going to be a challenge given the extent of Norse mythology and beliefs. But what Myrtle told us narrows it down some. Sten Klausen was Danish. I'll start by looking at the cults in Denmark."

James walked past me with the water bowl. "If it's all right, I'm gonna nurse Annie some more and work on getting the wards back up. Should probably bury another batch of Claymores too."

I wasn't overly enthused at the prospect of him handling explosives a mere few feet from me, but wanting a solid hour or two of concentration, I said, "Good idea," and opened the first book.

"How's it going, Prof?"

I didn't realize how dark it had gotten until James snapped on the light. Remarkably, the trailer's electricity still worked. I squinted at the open tomes spread over the table, then peered down at the notes I'd jotted into my legal pad. "Not as well as I'd hoped," I grumbled.

"Why? What's wrong?" He took the chair across from me. Annie padded under the table and licked one of my shoes before laying down. Being in the pit bull's good graces, while nice, did little to console my frustration.

"I've read up on all the cult practices for Hel in that region, but damned if I can find anything about the gold bracelet. Idols, sure. There's plenty about those, as well as details on human sacrifice and full-moon offerings. But nothing about bracelets—or even blondes, for that matter."

"Maybe the cult was secret," James suggested.

"Maybe, but that still leaves us shooting blind."

"There's nothing you can take from the other practices?"

I consulted my notes as James stood and made his way to the fridge. He returned with a couple of beers, cracking their caps and placing one of the bottles in front of me. I broke my own no-drinking rule and took a swallow. I needed something to ease the brain strain.

"Well, in every case, destroying the idol will destroy the god," I said.

James nodded. "There you go."

"And the protective circles across cults are pretty similar, salt being the most common medium."

James nodded some more in encouragement.

"But though some of the rites involve adorning the soon-to-be-sacrificed in jewelry," I said, "there's nothing about bracelets. I didn't even find anything resembling the symbol Carla drew for us."

"Still," James said, "two for three ain't bad. We'll deal with the bracelet thing when we come to it."

"*If* we come to it," I said. "Look, the ads were a great idea—I'm not saying they weren't—but what are the chances of the next victim, one, coming across the ad, and two, actually picking up a phone and—?"

The theme song to *The Good, the Bad and the Ugly* whistled from James's pants. He pulled his phone from his back pocket. After checking the number, he shrugged as if to say it wasn't in his contacts and raised the phone to his ear.

"Hello?"

Maybe this was Myrtle calling us back with information on who had purchased Sten's ranch at auction. But when he spoke again, his voice took on a velvety texture.

"Why, yes, it is," he said. "Can you describe the bracelet?"

I stood slowly, hands clasped together, not wanting to get my hopes up. There were probably more than a few women in Grimstone County desperate enough to respond to a personal ad that had nothing to do with them.

James snapped his fingers at me and nodded.

It's her, he mouthed.

10

"There she is," James said.

He had backed the Jeep into a space facing the front of the diner, and I craned my neck forward to see better. An elderly couple sat at a booth beside the plate-glass window, picking at their late dinners while a couple of trucker types hunched over the counter. A waitress with graying hair refilled their coffee.

"Looks a little old," I said.

"Not her, man. *Her.*" He rotated my head until I could see the young woman at the booth in the far corner. Her blond hair shifted over the shoulders of a pink sweater as she sipped from a glass of water and peered around. My gaze fell to the bracelet on her left wrist.

"Okay, good," I said, letting out a relieved breath. "Ready, Romeo?"

James grinned a little too broadly. "I was born for this kind of work. See you in five?"

"Yeah, I'll be at that second table from the booth. The small one. Just remember, I need time, so—"

"Keep her here as long as I can," James finished for me. "I know the drill, Prof. Watch and learn."

He climbed out of the Jeep and crossed the lot with a swagger. At my insistence, he'd lost the cowboy hat and swapped his vest for a leather jacket. I watched nervously as he entered the diner and made his way over to the young woman.

Her name was Allison. She had been wondering who'd given her the bracelet, a gift someone had wrapped in brown paper and left on her porch, and when she heard the ad on the radio, well, she just had to call and find out. James's idea had worked. He asked if they could meet to get to know one another, and Allison had suggested Pauline's Diner: "They have awesome steak burgers."

Now she straightened as James approached. He said something that made her break into a pretty smile. She stood and hugged him. James grinned at me over her shoulder and shot a little finger pistol.

"Focus, man," I muttered, but it looked as if he was off to a good start.

They sat across from one another, and for the next several minutes, I watched as she leaned forward, talking excitedly. For his part, James sat back, elbow perched on the back of the booth, throwing in a remark here and there. He'd assured me he'd be able to bullshit convincingly for however long it took me to assess the bracelet and remove it safely from her wrist.

When the five minutes were up, I took James's route through the diner. Allison was so transfixed on her conversation with him that she didn't so much as glance over. I took a seat at the table I'd pointed out, sitting so I had a view of James's face for communication purposes.

The waitress came over. "Coffee, hon?"

"Please," I said. "And that will be all." The last thing I needed was for her to hover. She returned a moment later and set the coffee down, along with a small bowl of sugar packets and cream cups.

"A shame about those missing girls, huh?"

"What?" I said, moving the coffee in front of me. "Oh, yeah."

"Been disappearing every month, regular like. Should be another one coming up."

When I looked up, I caught an excited gleam in her eyes. I nodded noncommittally, even though I was growing anxious. I needed to get started. I peeked over to see Allison leaning back with laughter, the bracelet shifting on her wrist. The waitress moved her wide hips over, blocking my view.

"What do you think's happening to them?" She then answered her own question. "Probably all sorts of awful things." She gave a shudder, but one that suggested pleasure rather than horror. Great. Not only did I have a hoverer, but a nutjob. I blew on my coffee and took a sip.

She lowered her voice to a whisper. "If you ask me, it's one of those Indians."

Did she know something we didn't? "The Utes? What makes you say that?"

"They're just creepy. No telling what they're up to out there on the reservation."

"You can't exactly get an arrest warrant on that, though, can you?"

The lines of her face furrowed in confusion before releasing around a loud bray of laughter. "I get it," she said. "That's funny!" She continued to laugh, her top teeth flaring from beneath her lip.

"It wasn't that funny," I muttered.

Her laughter wound down to a series of snorts. She wiped her nose on her sleeve and parked her right knee on the chair beside me. "You know, I haven't seen you around here before."

"I'm just in town for a few days, visiting a friend."

"Then what are you doing eating out alone?"

I was saved from having to invent an answer by the ding of a bell. James's and Allison's steak burgers were up. The waitress looked over at the pickup window, sighed, and pushed herself from the table. "Back to the grind," she muttered. "Let me know if you need anything else, hon."

The second she left, I shifted my sight to the astral level. The diner dimmed momentarily before a network of energies bloomed into view. I trained my focus on Allison's bracelet.

Damn, it was as bad as I'd feared. An ink-black energy was flowing from the metal and climbing her arm like a nest of tiny eels. The energy plunged into her ear where it circled her mind, ready to control her. Removing the cursed bracelet could drive her insane or kill her outright.

I'll have to be extra careful.

I reached into a coat pocket and retrieved a bag of salt. While the waitress was serving James and Allison their burgers, I sprinkled a protective circle around my chair, then set my cane beside my coffee. I avoided eye contact with the waitress as she returned past my table.

Okay, I thought, *time to see what you're made of.*

Angling the tip of the cane toward the bracelet, I incanted, creating a subtle link to the energy. The same sensations I'd experienced when I'd been yanked into the god's realm crept back into my awareness: the scent of death, the pull of greed.

I went still, ready to break the connection at the first sign of the goddess Hel. But this time she didn't seize my throat. The salt appeared to be doing its job. I took another breath and probed deeper.

The enchantment was originating from the bracelet's sigil. If I could deactivate it…

"Disfare," I whispered, sending out a quantum of the invocation as a test. But instead of dampening the sigil, the Word only seemed to animate it. The black energy coursing up Allison's arm began to wriggle and jump. She stopped mid-sentence and grasped her forehead.

James reached toward her. "Are you all right?"

"A migraine or something…" she replied, massaging her temples.

James looked over at me and turned up a hand in question. I shook my head to say I hadn't found a solution yet. Allison lowered her hand as the energy flowing from the bracelet normalized.

"That's weird," she said. "I'm not normally a migraine person."

"I hope *I* didn't trigger it," James said.

Allison laughed, and they resumed talking and eating. I pulled a piece of paper with some notes on it from a coat pocket and consulted it. Not knowing what kind of enchanted bracelet we were dealing with, I'd researched a range of them back at James's, compiling a list on how to release someone in their hold.

Deactivating the sigil was obviously out. It was too powerful, its hold on Allison too deep. For the same reason, I drew a mental slash through placing the sigil under my control. I was decades from that kind of power.

My eyes scanned further down, stopping on the final notation:

"As a last resort, the item might be tricked into releasing the enchantment."

Tricked, I thought. I was pretty decent with projection spells. If I could confuse the bracelet long enough, James might be able to pull it from Allison's wrist. She'd be free, and we'd have a powerful link to the perp.

I trained my focus on my left arm. *"Imitare,"* I said.

I repeated the Word several times, fashioning a three-dimensional likeness of my arm in my mental prism. When it appeared solid and convincing, I shifted my focus to the bracelet.

"Liberare," I said.

James's eyes widened as the projection of my forearm superimposed itself over his date's. I gestured at him to keep her distracted. He nodded quickly and started into a story that involved a lot of hand motion around his face. We needed to keep her from looking down.

On the astral plane, the enchantment stopped squirming. *Holy crap,* I thought, *this just might work.* Sensing a fresh presence inside the bracelet, the enchantment began to withdraw from Allison's mind to swarm my projection.

I waved to get James's attention, then pointed at the bracelet. I held up five fingers and began a countdown—something we'd worked out beforehand. When enough of the energy left her, James would pull the bracelet from her wrist.

I was to three when someone exclaimed, "What in the name of Sam Hill?"

The waitress had returned to refill James's and Allison's drinks and was staring down at Allison's arm where my projection hovered. Allison followed the waitress's gaze and let out a scream.

"Now!" I shouted to James.

The enchantment hadn't entirely released her, but we were looking at the best chance we would probably get. James lunged across the table, seizing Allison's wrist. When she realized what he was doing, she screamed again and began punching his hands. Grimacing, James worked his fingers around the bracelet's edges and pulled. The energy clamped down.

Thinking she was witnessing a robbery in progress, the waitress rushed James with the plastic pitcher of iced tea and broke it over his head. Tea and ice cubes rained everywhere. The commotion got the truckers' attention at the counter, who jumped up and began hustling over.

All right, this was going to hell in a hurry.

Sorry, buddy, but … "*Vigore!*" I shouted, aiming my cane at James.

The invocation landed against his chest, knocking him back. But the sudden force also overwhelmed the bracelet's hold on Allison, as I'd hoped. When James came to a rest, the bracelet was in his hands. Allison grunted and toppled over onto the seat. I prayed that enough of the energy had released her mind, but there was too much confusion to tell.

"What's going on?" one of the arriving truckers asked. He was a burly man with a thick black beard. His partner was just as big, but his beard was brown. Together, they looked like a pair of circus strongmen.

"They were making hand signals to one another," the waitress said excitedly. "And then he stole her bracelet. I think they're the ones who've been snatching those girls. Look, she's got blond hair like the others."

I stood and showed my hands. "No, no, we're actually working on the case. You can check with—"

Black Beard plowed a fist into my stomach. I doubled over with a breathless grunt. Another fist came down like a sledgehammer on my back. I grunted again and hit the floor. Work boots entered the fray, thudding against my sides. With Black Beard's next kick, I landed against the table where I'd been sitting. My coffee mug fell and shattered beside my head.

"Make him bleed!" the waitress screamed.

Luckily, my cane fell next, landing amid the broken shards of mug. I seized it between blows, swung the opal end toward Black Beard's face, and shouted a force invocation. In the heat of the moment, my calibration was off. I'd only meant to knock him down, but the force that caught him beneath the chin blasted him across the diner. The elderly couple didn't look over as he skidded past them on his back.

I pushed myself to my feet as James was hitting Brown Beard with a bolt from his wand. The silver energy spread around the big man like bailing wire, pinning his arms and legs together, shrinking his center of gravity. He swore loudly as he toppled over, flopping like a fish.

The waitress pulled a steak knife from her apron as she backed away from us. "You *are* them, aren't you?" she said, that strange excitement in her eyes again. "The kidnappers?"

I looked over at Allison, who was still down on the seat, then over at James. "This is going to look really bad, but we need to take her." He nodded and lifted her over his shoulder.

The waitress licked her lips. "Take me too."

"Forget it," James said, turning from her. "Freak."

The waitress stiffened in indignation, then narrowed her eyes at me. "I've got your descriptions. In a minute I'll have your vehicle and license plate number. I'll call the sheriff."

"Good," I said. "Tell Marge we'll be there in five."

I dropped a few bills on the table, counted them, and then took back the tip.

11

Allison sagged against me as James pulled up in front of the sheriff's station. He jogged around to my side of the Jeep, and I helped her into his arms. We had called ahead, and now Marge appeared at the front door.

"There's a couch back here," she said, leading the way.

James and I followed her into a break room. A table and small fridge took up one end. Marge wheeled a TV/VCR stand out of the way, and James set Allison on a plaid couch, resting the young woman's head carefully on the padded armrest. He covered her with a blanket.

"Is she going to be all right?" Marge asked.

"The shock of the bracelet coming off scored her mind a little," I said, looking down at Allison's pale face, "but fortunately it's nothing some healing magic can't cure. I infused her on the ride here. She'll sleep for a few hours, but when she wakes up, she should be fine. A little hung over, but fine."

"And she's safe?" Marge pressed.

"As long as the bracelet is off her, it can't compel her. She won't be victim number nine. Someone should stay with her, though."

"Franks will be back shortly," she said. "Where's the bracelet now?"

Careful to keep my fingers on its outer edges, I fished the bracelet from a bag of salt in my coat pocket and held it up. It was just as Carla had described: a thick band of old gold.

"The symbol is slightly different than what Carla drew," I said, tapping the scratching on the top of the bracelet. "But it's a moon sigil, used to activate an enchanted object on the full moon." I could sense the eel-like energy squirming beneath my fingers, searching for someone to compel. "I know you'll need the bracelet for evidence, but it still holds powerful magic. I'm going to ask that it stay with me and James until we can clean it."

I expected a fight from Marge; instead, she said, "Fine."

"Tell her what you told me in the Jeep," James said.

"Well, to get the bracelet off her, I projected my arm over hers, which confused the enchantment. It wasn't actually my arm—it was more like a hologram—but some of my energy was in that hologram."

Marge circled a hand to tell me to get to the point.

"Well, I could feel what the enchantment is designed to do. It directs the victim to a location."

"Where?" Marge asked.

"Possibly wherever the perp is. James and I could find out—with your permission, of course."

"Good, I'll go with you."

I groaned inwardly. That was always a problem when partnering with law enforcement. "Um, I don't think that's a good idea." I noticed James stepping back as Marge's flinty eyes narrowed menacingly. "Look, I'm just worried about the goddess showing up. James and I have the ability to handle something like that, especially now that we know what we're dealing with. The Grimstone County Sheriff's Department ... not so much."

"Shove it," she said. "If there's even the smallest chance the bracelet leads to the perp, I'm going to be there."

"You want an arrest, I get it," I said in frustration. "But what if we come face to face with a goddess of death, instead? Are you going to slap a pair of cuffs on her while reciting her Miranda rights?"

Marge drew herself up. "You getting smart with me?"

"No, it's an honest question. Nothing in your arsenal is effective against a god."

James chuckled nervously. "You know, Marge ... Everson sort of has a point."

She rounded on him. "Is that right, jackass?"

"How about this?" I said quickly. "Let James and me follow the enchantment, see where it leads. That's all. We'll report back as soon as we know something. See what you want to do."

Marge looked from James to me as though she'd bitten into something sour.

"That's partly why you consulted us," I reminded her. "To handle situations like this."

"And you've already gone behind my back once."

"It won't happen a second time," I said, hoping I could keep that promise.

"You get a location, you call me," she said at last.

"In the meantime..." I ventured.

"What?" she snapped.

"Well, Allison told James she found the bracelet on her doorstep packaged in brown paper. I don't know if you have any of the victims' trash in evidence, but similar packaging could give you a link to the perp. That will be useful if the enchantment doesn't lead us anywhere."

She pulled in her lips as though the information was setting off a fresh chain of ideas. Pulling out her phone, she made a call.

"Franks," she said. "I need you back here right now. *Now*," she repeated. "Forget the sobriety test. Call him a cab."

"We'll get going, then," I said before she could change her mind. "Thanks."

"Yeah, thanks, Marge," James said as he followed me out.

"Don't fuck this up," she called after us.

The sandy asphalt road rolled out under the Jeep's headlights as we left town and sped west across the desert. I held the bracelet in my lap, fingers on the pulse of its pull.

James peered over warily. "So, how are you not being attacked right now?"

"This is different than the hunting spell," I explained. "When I tapped into the scrunchie, I created a link between me and the girl's essence—which the goddess Hel had absorbed. That's how she got to me. With the bracelet, I'm not feeling the same connection."

"What are we following, then?"

"Some sort of homing beacon. The pull's coming in regular pulses."

"And this is where Allison would've been led?"

"I think so."

When the road curved, the moon shone into view, the barest sliver from being full. The goddess had lost her sacrifice, but that didn't mean the perp wouldn't find another one. We couldn't afford for this to be a dead end.

"Where does the road go?" I asked.

James nodded at a silhouette of rocky formations rising ahead of us. "Rattlesnake Hills. The old mining country."

"Sounds lovely."

When the Jeep began to climb, the pulse pulled us off onto a faint dirt road. The tires crunched through brush and over rocks, and rabbits scattered in the jouncing high beams. Before long, we arrived on a stone shelf. A pair of steep walls narrowed the way forward.

James slowed. "You sure about this, Prof?"

"If anything, the pulse is getting stronger. Hey, aim your lights over there."

James turned the wheel in the direction of my pointed finger and stopped as the wink of a red reflector became the rear of a compact car. "Holy shit," James said. He rolled forward some more. Additional cars shone into view. They were lined up beneath a large rock overhang, as though the space were a small parking garage. Aerial searches wouldn't have spotted them.

"I'm guessing these belong to the women?" James said.

"Either that or someone's trying to hide his car collection from his wife."

I heard James counting them quietly. Eight vehicles, eight victims. That's why the sheriff's department had found no evidence of foul play at the victims' homes. Under the control of the bracelets, the women had all gotten into their cars and essentially abducted themselves.

"Is this when we call Marge?" he asked.

"Not quite yet. Let's turn the Jeep around and park it."

Using what probably would have been Allison's space,

James performed a three-point turn and then killed the lights and engine. I gripped my cane and got out of the Jeep. James joined me around back, wand drawn.

"The pulse leads up there," I said, pointing up one of the rock faces.

"Illuminare," James commanded. A silver ball of light appeared from the tip of his wand. With a snap of his wrist, James sent it in the direction I'd indicated. The glowing ball illuminated a series of steps cut into the rock face. Twenty feet higher, the steps terminated at a hole.

"An old prospecting tunnel," James said.

"And it's exactly where the bracelet's telling us to go," I muttered above my tightening chest.

"Oh, right. Your phobia thing."

I hated that word, but yeah, my phobia of being underground was already speeding my heart rate and thinning my breaths.

"Is *this* when we call Marge?" he asked.

"I don't want her going in there," I said. "Not until we've checked it out first."

"And if this goddess Hel shows up?"

"Hopefully we find and destroy the idol before that happens. If not, I brought one of the potions I had you cook." I removed the small bottle from my pocket and gave it a little shake. "It's a sleeping potion, which should work on a god of her caliber. Give us time to clear out."

James opened the Jeep's rear door and unlocked his metal gun compartment as the ball of light returned to hover overhead. I watched him swap out the ammo in his Peacemakers for salt cartridges, then do the same with his shotgun, pumping the action to load the first shell.

"For insurance," he explained, slinging the shotgun strap over a shoulder and closing the doors.

I nodded. It couldn't hurt. We ascended the narrow stone steps and then stopped on either side of the prospecting tunnel. James sent the orb into the opening, and we peered inside. The tunnel was about four feet wide and tall enough for both of us to stand in.

"One-way trip, I guess," James whispered, pointing. Near the entrance, several sets of shoeprints tracked through the sand, but none came back out.

"Watch your step," I said as I entered, keeping my stance wide so as not to disturb the prints.

I followed the orb as it illuminated the rough-hewn walls stretching ahead. After thirty feet, the tunnel ended. A hole with a timber ladder plunged into the darkness. James dropped the illumination orb inside. A draft of cold, foul air blew past us as we looked down.

James recoiled, the back of a hand to his nose. "Jesus. That can't be good."

I steeled myself against the rotten-meat odor as my eyes tracked the descending orb. A sequence of horizontal tunnels glowed in and out of view. Only after the orb had gone the equivalent of several stories did the bracelet pulse hard beneath my fingers. I pocketed the bracelet and slid my cane through my belt, then took several deep breaths to force my chest open.

"You ready?" I asked.

The rungs of the ladder were old and slick with moisture as we descended. Rusted cables ran along one side. Somewhere beneath us, air moaned through a flue of tunnels, pushing up more of the foul stench. We got off at the side tunnel indicated by the bracelet. I shivered in the orb's silver light, but the deepening cold felt more psychic than physical.

The smell was much stronger down here, too.

"Hey," James whispered as the orb wandered ahead, "what did you think of Allison?"

"I think she's really lucky we reached her in time."

"That's not what I meant. What do you think of her as, you know, a woman?"

"Huh?"

"Back in the diner, I felt like we were really starting to connect."

I shook my head and began following a set of metal cart tracks, the bracelet tugging me forward.

"I mean, she's pretty," James said, hustling to catch up, "but she's also super nice. I haven't dated a lot of nice girls. She volunteers her Saturday mornings at a soup kitchen. A soup kitchen, man."

"What happened to the librarian?" I asked thinly.

"What happened? *You* happened."

"What's that supposed to mean?"

"Oh, come off it, bro. I saw the way you and Myrtle were looking at each other."

"One, we weren't looking at each other in any *way*. And, two, you need to focus."

"You should totally go for it. I would. Oh, hey, watch your head."

I turned back in time to run face-first into an ore chute. In the clanging echo, I swore and rubbed my forehead. Rock debris spilled from the chute over my shoes, creating more noise. "Look," I hissed, "we're here to stop a god, not swap relationship advice. Now drop it!"

"Last question. Would it be inappropriate to ask Allison

on a second date?"

I ignored him and continued walking, past side tunnels, piles of timber, and old mining equipment. In an alcove, I glanced over a work bench littered with large bolts. A wooden box from the Atlas Powder Company sat to one side. While James inspected the box, I opened a browning edition of the *Grimstone Star*. It was dated June 1904, evidently when the mining tunnel was last active.

"There's some old dynamite in here," James said, tipping the box toward him with a boot.

"Then maybe you shouldn't be doing that."

He shrugged and withdrew his foot. I threw up a shield as the box landed hard against the ground. When no explosion followed, I dispelled the shield and glared at James. He didn't seem to notice.

"You think the women really came this far down?" he asked.

I swallowed back my irritation. At least he was talking about the case again. "If the bracelet was compelling them, yes." I turned the band of gold around in my fingers. "The pull is really strong now."

"Hold on," James said, peering past me. "I think there's a light down there." With a Word, he killed the illumination orb. The tunnel fell into total darkness—save for a soft glow that highlighted an opening farther down.

"Keep the orb off and follow me," I whispered.

With James holding the back of my coat, we made our way toward the light. We arrived at the opening, which led onto a cavernous room where a large vertical shaft had been drilled into the ceiling. A column of pale moonlight fell from overhead, illuminating what looked like a shrine on the far side of the room. The bracelet tugged me toward it, the smell of decomposition overpowering now. I withdrew the stoppered bottle with the sleeping potion.

"Cover me," I whispered.

James nodded and drew his Peacemakers. As I made my way across the floor, my eyes began to adjust. I glanced around the walls of the room before refocusing on the shrine. Urns had been arranged on either side of a cross, its horizontal section comprised of two sticks that formed an X.

At the cross's crux hung a second gold band—the bracelet's twin and the source of the beacon. I could feel the two bracelets working on me, pulling me toward the shrine. A discordant hum picked up between them, and they began to rattle.

"Careful, Prof," James whispered.

When I looked down, I was already in the column of moonlight, the floor around my shoes marred with blood and gobbets of rotting tissue. I raised my eyes. In the dark recesses behind the shrine, body parts were scattered. Some looked fresher, others drawn and leathery. A set of dusty bones, probably going back to the women Sten had disappeared, lay in a pile.

Off to the left, a pair of stove-in eyes stared out at me in desperation. I recognized the head as belonging to the very latest victim.

The bracelet gave a final hard pulse, and I bit back a shout. A signal?

The air in the room dropped several degrees, chilling my sweat-soaked shirt, and a low moan sounded. I wheeled around to find a monstrous figure shambling toward me. Dropping the bracelet, I fumbled to unstopper the potion. Shots flashed from James's revolvers, their explosions reverberating through the killing chamber as the figure seized me.

12

Cold fingers closed around my throat and lifted me from my feet. I gagged and seized the being's wrist with one hand, potion clenched in the other. I'd been unable to open it, and James had stopped shooting, probably for fear of hitting me. It didn't seem the salt rounds had been effective anyway.

This could be bad, I thought.

A horrible stink of death broke against my face as the being drew me in close. Large eyes glowed pale in the moonlight, their pupils covered in a milk-white caul. The right one was brown with old blood where the witch had wounded it. This was the goddess Hel— had to be.

I kicked feebly at the giantess's stomach as I struggled to breathe. Fingers caressed my hair, then stopped suddenly.

"Who are you?" she moaned in a rattling bass voice.

That fact that I was neither blond-haired nor a woman seemed to arouse confusion, then anger. The grip around my throat tightened, mashing bone and cartilage. I threw the bottle at the goddess, needing it to break against her and release the sleeping potion, but it only bounced from her forehead and fell to the ground.

I seized Hel's wrist in both hands, straining for the thinnest slip of air. Dark clouds drifted over my vision.

"Where's my tribute?" she groaned.

A silver cord streaked through the growing dimness and lassoed the being's throat.

"Allison sends her apologies, but she couldn't make it." James grunted as he tugged his light invocation. Hel staggered backward, her grip around my neck faltering. "Hope you don't mind a pair of dudes instead."

The goddess's face turned toward James—and was met by a rock-salt blast from his Winchester. She bellowed and released me. I crashed to the shrine, urns toppling beneath me. Blond hair and vital organs spilled from them. I seized the potion and backpedaled, my ears ringing from the gunshot.

Hel groped toward James, smoke rising from her face. My partner unloaded another blast, this one into her chest, and pumped the gun again. The goddess recoiled—more in shock than pain, it seemed. She wasn't used to her victims fighting back. That advantage wouldn't last, though.

"We need to get out of here," I called hoarsely.

In the commotion, James didn't hear me. With his next blast, Hel barely flinched. She grabbed his shotgun by the barrel, wrenched it from James's grip, and flung it aside. He switched to his Peacemakers, the cavern erupting as he fired them alternately. I unstoppered the potion with my teeth, drew my cane, and ran at the goddess as she reached down for him.

James re-holstered his spent revolvers and drew his wand. *"Protezione!"* he called.

A crackling shield grew around him but dissolved into sparks as Hel punched a hand through. James shouted another Word. Silver energy spun from his wand, pinning Hel's arms to her sides. The invocation's bright light illuminated her entire form for the first time.

I stopped, my potion arm cocked.

We weren't dealing with a goddess. The being staring down at us from beneath tangled hanks of black hair was a dude. Death had turned his skin a pale blue and swelled his fish-belly lips. When he strained against the web, his tattered robes trembled, sending off horrid waves of death stink.

"Everson," James said, backing away. "What the hell is that?"

Not Hel, that was clear. Everything about the being's appearance screamed zombie, and yet I could feel god-like power emanating from him.

With a grunt, the being broke from James's manifestation and lashed a hand out, snagging a corner of his jacket. I rushed forward and splashed the being with the potion. Pink fumes plumed up around him, giving James the opportunity to wriggle from the arms of his jacket to freedom. But though the being staggered through the mist, he didn't appear on the verge of dropping off to sleep.

I aimed my cane and called, *"Vigore!"* The force scattered against the being as though he were a brick wall, barely shaking him.

This is pointless, I thought. *We need to locate the power source and destroy it. And I'm not feeling it down here.*

"Let's go!" I shouted to James.

He nodded as I ran past him. He'd retrieved his shotgun and was backpedaling to get off another blast. I heard the click-clack of the pump, then the violent explosion. "Shit," he panted, hustling to catch up. "That didn't do anything."

"No amount of salt will." I called light to my cane as we hit the tunnel. "We need to find the idol."

"I'm not going back in there."

"Don't think it's there," I said. "It's with whoever's summoning that thing."

The tunnel walls shook as the being gave chase. I peered over a shoulder to find his milky eyes glowing from the darkness, growing larger. He was moving too fast. We'd never outrace him.

Silver light flashed as James cast back a missile-like force invocation. Rock debris exploded around the being, but he barely broke stride. The images of the rotting body parts at the shrine jagged through my mind. We'd be joining the collection if we couldn't slow him down. Up ahead, the alcove with the work bench glowed into view. Underneath was our answer.

"Dynamite," I panted. "Can you…?"

"Hell yes," James said. "Just be ready for some serious heat."

As we sprinted past the alcove, James aimed his wand at the box of dynamite and release a thundering *"Forza dura!"*

The box burst into splinters. My shield took shape around us an instant before the ear-numbing explosion that followed. A violent plume of fire and dust swallowed the being and knocked the spherical shield that encased us forward like a hamster ball. At our backs, the tunnel shook and collapsed.

Our bouncing motion inside the ball became so violent that I couldn't hold the manifestation. The shield burst apart, and James and I tumbled to a stop. I lay still for a moment, listening to the clacks of rocks from the collapse behind us. My head reeled when I sat up.

"You all right?" I asked, coughing.

"Sure, let's do that again," he mumbled. His wand glowed silver, revealing his dusty rock-cut face and pile of mussed hair. He retrieved one of his revolvers from the ground and tossed me my cane.

"So, did that finish him?" he asked.

"Slowed him," I replied, staggering to my feet. "And something tells me it won't be for long."

As if on cue, the tunnel rumbled and we both looked back. Large rocks shifted and spilled from the collapse. The being was trying to unbury himself.

James and I limp-ran toward the ladder and scrambled up the incline shaft. We reached the entrance tunnel and made our way down the stone steps and past the victims' cars, not slowing until we'd arrived at the Jeep.

"His power may not extend beyond the mine," I said of the being as we climbed in.

"*May* not?" James shook his head, fired the engine, and stomped the gas. I kept my eyes fixed on the side mirror as the Jeep roared and jumped down the track we'd arrived by. But nothing was pursuing us.

Minutes later, James slewed out onto the asphalt road and accelerated to eighty.

"Can I assume that wasn't Hel?" he said.

Even while we'd been fleeing, my analytical mind had been cycling through the Norse myths, trying to figure out just who or what the being had been. I now had a working theory.

"Remember how I mentioned that if a god remains dead

for too long, they lose a lot of their faculties, become zombie-like?"

"Yeah...?" James said.

"That's because when gods die in mythology, they don't really die. They go to an underworld where they sort of ... hang out. Through powerful rituals, humans can still communicate with them, and some can even call them up. But they're not the same. It explains the deathly appearance and odor of what we just confronted, as well as why the potion couldn't put him to sleep."

"So which god are we talking about?"

"That particular cross at the shrine means we're still dealing with the Norse pantheon. And the only god who would be in the underworld, at least according to some of the cult myths, is Gorr, the god of wealth. He's actually the god I mentioned earlier, the one Hel refused to release."

"Wealth," James said reflectively. "Hey, didn't Myrtle say that guy from the early 1900s was in deep debt?"

I snapped my fingers and pointed at him. "That's right. He or his parents may have been active in a Norse cult back in Denmark, some of which lasted into the previous century. Probably how he obtained the idol. Followers would have been warned against attempting to summon Gorr, especially since human sacrifice had fallen out of favor long before then, but if Sten was desperate enough, he just might have seen it as his only chance."

"But he was a mortal, right?"

"As far as we know, yeah."

"Then how'd he pull it off? I mean, those types of summonings get you a demon ninety-nine times out of a hundred. I'm having to deal with that crap at the communes every other day, it seems."

"Myrtle also mentioned the Great Quake of 1902," I said. "Big seismic events have been known to disrupt the interface between worlds, making them more permeable. That could explain Sten's success in calling up a god. The permeability we talked about last night would explain why the god's back."

"A zombie god," James said, shaking his head. "So, what's our move, Prof?"

"We still have to find the idol and destroy it. That much hasn't changed."

James's cell phone began to whistle. He checked the number, smiled, and raised the phone to his ear. "Hey there, Myrtle," he said in a smooth, country voice. "Huh?" He glanced over at me with a sudden frown. "He's actually busy right now, is there something I can pass on?"

I grasped for the phone. Myrtle's search may have turned up something. James pushed my hands away and switched ears. He listened for the next minute, brow furrowed in concentration. I strained to hear what Myrtle was saying, but the roar of the motor drowned out her voice.

"Are you sure?" James asked. "All right, I'll let Everson know." He ended the call and turned toward me. "Good news. It took a while, but she was able to find the records dealing with the auction of Sten's property."

"And...?" I asked, almost breathless. Whoever had acquired Sten's property would also have acquired the idol.

"Does the name Brunhold ring a bell?" he teased. "Brunhold Development, specifically?"

"The dwarves?"

James nodded. "Myrtle thinks they were interested in a mining claim Sten held, but they bid on everything—house, personal property, you name it. And there's more. You remember that guy we met on the way to the library, the one who had words with you?"

"Taffy?"

"He's the one who signed the certificates of title."

"Meaning he took possession of the idol," I concluded.

I thought about that. If Taffy had learned what the idol could do, he might have had no compunction about sacrificing young women to deepen his family's fortunes. Dwarves had an innate lust for riches, after all—as well as a natural ability to handle powerful magic.

"I'll call Marge," James said, already scrolling for the number, "fill her in."

I slapped the phone out of his hand.

"Hey! What was that for?"

"I know what I promised Marge, but listen. We denied the zombie god his sacrifice, but remember what happened to Sten? If the perp wants to survive the full-moon cycle, he's going to have to find Gorr another young blond. That means we have to get to the idol, like thirty minutes ago. And we have a good idea where it is now. But if we let Marge in the loop, everything grinds to a halt. She'll call us off while she requests a search warrant from a judge who may or may not believe in god summonings. We can't take that chance. No time."

"Do you know the kind of crap you're going to land me in?" James asked, rooting a hand between the door and seat where his phone had fallen. "I'm on her shit list as it is."

"Not if we nail the perp and stop the killings tonight."

James retrieved his phone. He looked from the glowing screen to the full moon, then sighed and pushed the phone into his pocket. "I thought I was supposed to be the one who broke the rules."

"Yeah, well, there's smart rule-breaking and dumb rule-breaking. If I can get you committing more of the first than the second, I've done my job. I never claimed to be a saint."

"I'm the one who has to live out here," he complained.

"Well, if it's any consolation, I'm on plenty of shit lists back in Manhattan."

James shook his head, then snorted a laugh, which told me he was on board.

"You won't regret it," I said. "Now, what can you tell me about the dwarves' compound?"

"That's the thing, it's huge. Looking for the idol in there will be like trying to find a needle in a haystack ... if that haystack were full of battle axes and pissed-off dwarves."

"That's where Taffy's desperation to appease Gorr becomes an advantage," I said. "We find Taffy, and there's a really good chance we'll find the idol."

"And how are we gonna find Taffy?"

"We'll use his fluid to cast a hunting spell." When James frowned at me in question, I showed him the shoulder of my coat. "Remember when he grabbed me through the window? His palm was soaked in sweat. Meaning his essence is in the fabric. It's just a matter of drawing it out."

James chuckled. "Man, you are *definitely* no saint. In fact, you could be the devil himself."

"And the devil loves company," I said, punching him in the shoulder.

13

"That place is huge," I whispered.

"I tried to warn you," James whispered back. "The dwarves don't mess around. Took them decades to build, and they're always adding to it. I've heard the compound extends underground too."

From between the boulders that concealed us, I peered up at the stone fortress dominating the desert bluff. The walls that rose five or six stories were windowless, with stark cornices and powerful square pillars carved from the gray stone. From our vantage point partway up the bluff, we had a good view of the main gate. Its metal doors were closed. We had stopped at James's place en route, and the hunting spell I'd prepared tugged in my hand now, insisting our target, Taffy, was inside. The only question was how to get to him.

I checked my watch. Almost eleven. "Do you think they're all in for the night?"

James shrugged. "Your guess is as good as mine, though I've seen them out and about at all hours. They like to drink."

"Any others entrances?"

"No doubt, but good luck finding them."

He was right. Dwarves were notoriously good at creating doors that blended into the stone around them. Not even a reveal spell could expose them. And dwarves often disguised their most important doors further with old enchantments. I eyed the fortress again. When faced with a similar obstacle recently, I'd used a force invocation to vault up to a rampart, but this fortress had no rampart. The compound was completely enclosed.

But we *had* to get inside, dammit.

I was considering our options when the revving and grinding of an engine grew in my hearing. James and I peered down. A pair of headlights was swerving its way up the winding road to the compound.

"Bottoms up?" James asked, reaching inside his vest for the stealth potion we'd cooked and funneled into water bottles the night before. I nodded quickly and grabbed my own potion.

"Might be our best chance." I unscrewed the cap on my bottle and forced down the sludge-like liquid while James alternately gagged and swore. In his defense, it was an acquired taste.

"Let's go," I said, gripping my cane and maneuvering around the boulders in a low stoop.

James followed me up the bluff toward where the paved road met the front gate. Emphasizing that this was a stealth mission, I had discouraged him from carrying his guns and absolutely forbidden explosives, which I'd caught him stowing in the Jeep. As we climbed now, I could hear his empty holsters slapping against his hips, though the sound grew fainter, as if he were falling behind. When I glanced around, James was still at my back but nearly indistinguishable from his surroundings. The potion was doing its job.

We arrived at the gate ahead of the car and hunkered on the side where the headlights wouldn't hit us.

"This is wild," James said, his voice seeming to arrive from a great distance. Against the stone wall, he was practically invisible. I could just make out his outline, but only because I was looking for him.

"It won't last," I reminded him. "We'll need to be in and out in roughly thirty."

I hunkered lower as the car, a yellow Hummer, swung into view. It approached us crookedly, then slowed while great locks clunked inside the gate. As the gate's two doors began to open inward, I tugged James's vest. Staying low, we stole into the compound just behind the Hummer.

While the vehicle continued along the drive, I pulled James into an especially dark shadow beside the closing gate. I needed a moment to take stock of the compound's layout.

The Hummer entered what looked like a courtyard, headlights shining over a central pool. Handsome buildings of stone rose around it, some as high as the compound itself. I felt like I was inside a cave, which I supposed was the point. The only lights to be seen were in an occasional narrow window.

"Where to?" came James's barely audible voice.

I refocused on my cane. The hunting spell was tugging us toward an especially large building on the far side of the courtyard. I withdrew my coat strap, knotted it around a belt loop, and handed the other end of the strap to James, something I'd meant to do outside.

"Stay close," I said.

I made my way down the drive, James right behind. Loud laughter sounded from one building and arguing that was just as loud from another. Someone on a top floor blasted metal music. It wasn't until we'd reached the courtyard that I noticed a pair of red eyes glowing faintly halfway up the side of a building.

James grunted as I shoved him against a wall. From the deep shadows, I squinted back at the eyes until a slender, six-foot silhouette took shape around them. Crap. A giant lizard. And it wasn't alone.

More lizards scurried up and down the sides of buildings, pausing to bob their heads and grunt to one another. Dwarves were known to employ the creatures for mountain transport, but in this case, they were probably being used as night sentries. The lizards possessed a range of keen senses—hopefully all accounted for by our stealth potion.

"We cool?" James asked in my ear.

I felt over James's face until I found his lips and pressed a finger against it.

One of the lizards had cocked its head. I looked from it to what seemed a growing number of their kind. Were they converging on us? Or was I just noticing them all for the first time?

I gauged our distance to our target building—about thirty yards away—and tugged for James to follow.

We set off at a fast walk, my eyes jumping from building to building. The lizards grunted back and forth and scurried lower. It was as if they knew *something* was in their midst but couldn't make out what or where.

One dropped into the courtyard in front of us. I veered left and felt James stumble to keep up. The lizard raised its spiny head. A tongue thick enough to fell a man flickered from its mouth, revealing a set of impressive teeth. I didn't want to find out what those felt like.

As more lizards dropped into the courtyard behind us, I seized James's arm and broke into a run. We reached the building and raced up a short flight of steps. Behind us, the lizards' grunts rose into high, echoing calls. Padded toes raced toward us over the flagstones. I tried the door handle—unlocked, thank God—and James and I pushed our way inside.

We closed the heavy oak door just as a tongue thudded against it. Silver light flashed from James's wand, sealing the entrance with a locking spell.

"Sweet Jesus," he breathed.

More thuds hit the wood, but the spell held. Getting out of the compound was going to be another story, but we'd cross that bridge when we came to it—as James would say. Right now, we had an idol to destroy.

We'd arrived in a large room with an array of pedestals, on top of which stood busts of long-bearded dwarves. No doubt Taffy's lineage.

The hunting spell pulled me toward a pair of stone stairways that climbed to a second story galley. At the top of the steps, my cane pivoted to the right where, at the end of a hallway, light glowed beneath a door. My cane began jerking like a live wire.

Taffy was inside.

Tapping James's shoulder for him to cover me, I crept forward past mounted axes and shields. The doorknob turned in my hand, and I eased the door open.

The room was a large, messy office. At the far end, Taffy sat at a desk, his broad back to me. He'd stripped down to a white tank top, the jacket I'd seen him wearing earlier that day draped over the back of his chair. In the light of a desk lamp, his hairy shoulders bulged as he muttered over something.

The idol?

Before I could steal forward to find out, the phone on his desk rang. Taffy lifted the handset, grunted something in a Dwarfish dialect, listened, then grunted again.

Hanging up the phone, he took the thing he'd been muttering over and stuffed it into a pocket, then pushed himself from his chair and reached down to grasp a leather-bound handle. It was attached to a war hammer. As he raised it, silver light flashed in my peripheral vision.

"Wait!" I shouted at James, but the faint warning was too late.

James had unleashed an invocation, binding the dwarf in a net of silver energy. Until that point, Taffy hadn't been aware of our presence. The phone call had likely been to inform him that the lizards had picked up what might or might not have been an intruder around his building and to suggest he investigate. We'd still had the advantage of stealth.

"*Had*" being the operative term.

Taffy roared as the silver cords bound his arms. The hammer dropped from his grip and landed on the stone floor with a resounding clang, sending out a massive shockwave. I was blown backward, past toppling furniture and books cascading from shelves. I landed beside the door we'd entered, sharp pain flaring through my left arm. Rotating the shoulder to make sure it hadn't dislocated, I turned to where James was groaning. Besides being able to hear my partner, I could see him a little more clearly. He winced and rubbed the back of his head.

"The hell was that?"

"Take a wild guess," I said.

While Taffy struggled against his restraints, the war hammer at his feet warped the surrounding air with energy.

"Enchanted weapon?" he ventured.

"Yeah, and it just blew a chunk of the stealth magic from our systems."

Which meant there wasn't any time to lose. Recovering my cane, I rose to my feet and stumbled toward the lump in Taffy's pants pocket. (Not *that* one, you pervs.) It was the same size as the idol around Sten's neck in the newspaper photo.

But I'd only made it a few steps when the silver light dissolved from Taffy's body. I swore. Dwarves and their damned resistances to magic. Taffy lifted the huge hammer. Red-faced and shaking, he scanned his office.

"Who the devil are you?" he demanded. "Show yourself!"

His short-sightedness was compensating for our fading potion. I stopped and drew my sword slowly from my staff. If I couldn't get to the idol, perhaps a precise force invocation could.

But Taffy didn't give me a chance. With a roar, he swung the hammer in a blind arc.

Throwing up my staff, I shouted, *"Protezione!"*

The shield that bloomed from the staff met the hammer's shockwave in an explosion of sparks. Jarring pain shot down my staff arm, and I skidded back several feet. James wasn't as lucky. Still recovering from the last wave, the force lifted him partway up the wall and dropped him on his head.

I turned back to Taffy. He'd yet to draw an exact bead on us, but it would only take one more shockwave to expose us, even with his poor vision. It was now or never.

I aimed the tip of my sword at his bulging pocket and drew the sword back with a shouted *"Vigore!"*

But instead of tearing the pocket open as I'd hoped, the force invocation broke his brass fasteners, and his pants dropped to his ankles. Taffy looked down at his tighty whities and back up. Tears of rage shone in his eyes, and his apple-red cheeks deepened to a furious shade of scarlet.

Yanking his pants up his stubby legs with one hand, he brought the war hammer against the floor with the other. Even with my shield in place, the shockwave lifted me from my feet.

"Aw, crap," James complained as he was upended again.

"Y-you!" Taffy shouted, looking from James to me. "And you!"

Yeah, we were fully visible now. Taffy stalked forward, one hand balling up the side of his pants.

"We know about the idol," I said quickly while backing away. "We know that the god got out of your control, that you didn't mean for those women to be hurt. If you give us the idol, we can end this tonight."

Casting the perpetrator as the victim sometimes worked, but Taffy was beyond reason, beyond words even. He let out a barbaric cry as he drew his war hammer back.

Before he could swing it again, four silver bolts corkscrewed in, landing with explosive force against the dwarf's head and chest. I followed up James's assault with a force blast that sunk his paunch. Taffy grunted, but rather than slow him, our magic only seemed to infuriate him further. Spittle flew from his ginger-bearded lips as he reset his slipper-clad feet and charged.

With a rapid incantation, my light shield encircled Taffy's head. *If I can cut off his air, I might be able to stop him.*

The dwarf's red-flecked eyes bulged, but he kept coming. He swung again. This time, James arrested the war hammer with a silver net of energy. Taffy struggled against it, his face turning from scarlet to blue. I gritted my teeth to maintain the shield, which was starting to waver around the dwarf's neutralizing energy. But before my magic could come apart, Taffy ran out of oxygen.

He mouthed a string of choice words, most of them directed at me, then collapsed.

I released the shield while James moved the war hammer out of Taffy's reach and bound him in silver cords. At the dwarf's slumped body, I dug into his front pockets. My fingers closed around something smooth and wooden.

Salting and burning the idol would destroy Gorr and close the portal to the Norse underworld—our mission would be complete—but when my hand emerged, it was holding a wooden pipe. I turned out his other pockets in disbelief, then rifled his desk. I found notebooks and transaction records with the Brunhold Development and Realty logos, but nothing even remotely cultish. There was only carbon dust and a metal reamer on the desktop.

He'd been cleaning his damned pipe.

"These are all real estate books," James said, kicking through the thick tomes that had fallen during our battle on his way toward me. He picked up the pipe I'd set on the desk and sniffed the bowl. "Just tobacco ash," he said in what sounded like disappointment.

If *I* had failed to appease a homicidal god and would be dead unless I found him a replacement sacrifice, would I be at home in my undershirt, cleaning my pipe? The answer, of course, was no.

"Shit," I spat. "Taffy's not our perp."

Beside me, James was looking at his smartphone. "Shit is right. Marge has called me a ton of times." His eyes slid over, asking if *now* was the time to contact her. I was considering how I was ever going to explain this to the sheriff when the door downstairs banged open.

"I thought you sealed it," I hissed.

"With Taffy here sucking up all my magic, I had to borrow from the locking spell to launch that final attack." He scratched the back of his neck. "Guess I forgot to put it back."

I shook my head, but the truth was we were here because of me. Footsteps climbed the stairs. If our arriving company was even half as volatile as Taffy, we were about to have our hands full. With a pair of invocations, I closed and locked the office door, then wheeled in search of an escape.

"No windows or doors," James said. "I already checked."

"Well, isn't that nice."

I backed from the door toward the desk, sword and staff raised. I didn't want another fight, but I doubted the dwarves were going to give us a choice. They had every right to defend their turf. We were intruders after all. And hell, we'd just KO'd one of their family members. Something told me they weren't going to allow us the breath to explain ourselves.

The door shook.

"If they get through," I said, "well, *when* they get through, let me do the talking."

The door shook again. James backed up beside me. I adjusted my slick grip on my sword and staff, waiting for the blade of a battle axe to cleave the wood.

"Croft!" someone shouted. "Wesson!"

James peered over at me, his face the color of ash. It was Marge. And by her tone, I think we would both have preferred the dwarves.

"Crap," I muttered.

14

I released the locking spell, and the door banged open. Marge stood in the doorway in her sheriff's tans and a brown coat. A small army of bearded dwarves murmured at her back. Marge limped inside and glared around the trashed office. A slender crack ran the length of the stone floor, courtesy of Taffy's hammer blow.

I watched Marge's eyes follow the crack to the dwarf, who remained slumped over, his pants around his hairy shins. Her frown deepened. "What did you two do to him?"

James began to stutter, but I showed him a hand.

"This is all my fault," I said. "The bracelet led us to an old mine. James wanted to call you when we got there, but I insisted we check it out first, make sure it wasn't dangerous. We found the victims inside. Their corpses, anyway. And then something attacked us. A zombie god."

"But you're no longer *at* the mine," Marge said, her eyes narrowing dangerously.

"That's true," I said. "After we escaped, we received information suggesting the idol was here. Once more James wanted to call you, but I overruled him. With time running short, I felt that finding and destroying the idol was our priority. I broke my promise. I went renegade."

I'd always wanted to say that last line, but it came out sounding apologetic and weak.

"'Cause you thought the sheriff's department would just get in the way," Marge said bitterly. She sucked her teeth, her salty blue eyes squinting at me in a way that could have curdled milk.

Taffy coughed and sat up. Two of the dwarves attended to him while the six or so others straightened up the office. For the first time, it occurred to me that only a few minutes had elapsed between us triggering the lizard alarm and Marge arriving. Way too short a time for her to have responded to a call from the dwarves.

"How did you find us here?" I asked.

"Think I'm stupid? I had Deputy Franks tail you. He was reporting back on your whereabouts. When he saw you staking out the compound, I knew I had to haul ass over here before you two got yourselves into trouble. I underestimated how quickly that would happen."

Ouch, I thought, but she was right. I had screwed things up royally.

Marge had opened her mouth—to render our punishments, no doubt—when James spoke up.

"Hey, guys?" He'd been standing off to one side, messing with his phone. Now he activated the speaker and held it toward us. "There's something you should hear."

"Hi, it's Myrtle again," the recorded voice said. *"Listen, I had a total brain fart earlier. Everson asked about Sten's personal*

effects too, and those wouldn't have been auctioned but held at the jail. I searched the old jail records and found an entry about six months after his death. Apparently, his ex-wife returned to Grimstone with her children and new husband. She signed for the articles that were in Sten's possession when he was arrested. Her remarried name was Clara Fratelli. Anyway, I hope that helps."

I repeated the name as James put the phone away. "Fratelli. Isn't that Elmer's last name? The guy who does odd jobs at the lot?"

"It is," Marge said, "and that jibes with something *I* found. While you two were out playing Dukes of Hazard, I went back over the surveillance footage at Lot C. About two days before Dawn's disappearance, Elmer entered their break building and came back out ninety-one seconds later. It wouldn't have looked suspicious except that Allison told you her bracelet had been wrapped in brown paper. Well, guess what Elmer had in the pocket of his coveralls?"

"A small brown package?" I asked.

"What looked like the edge of one," Marge said. "And it was gone when he came out. The girls keep lockers in that building. I can't think of a better place to leave Dawn something where only she would find it."

"'We begin by coveting what we see every day,'" I quoted, thinking about the injury to Elmer's right eye. "Is he under arrest?" I asked Marge quickly. "We need to destroy the idol."

"I'm going to make the arrest now," she said. "But you're both coming with me."

"We are?" James and I asked almost simultaneously.

Behind us, Taffy released a roar. He had recovered and, judging by the murder in his eyes, had a sharp short-term memory. A pair of dwarves seized him by the arms while a third grabbed him around the waist.

"I'm gonna destroy you!" he grunted up at us. "I'm gonna tear your limbs off, then use them to beat your bodies bloody! I'm gonna stomp your skulls in!"

He struggled against the restraining dwarves, managing to shuffle his feet forward a few inches before more dwarves joined in. Together they spun Taffy onto the backs of his heels and dragged him from the room, additional promises of violence trailing behind him.

"You're the experts in magic," Marge explained when the commotion died down. "And you're right. That's part of the reason I consulted you, to help with situations like this. You've got tools and know-how we don't." She raised a threatening finger. "But that doesn't mean your assess aren't getting skinned for tonight. You're gonna learn one way or another."

Her prosthetic leg gave a harsh squeak as she pivoted on it and paced from the room.

James and I followed, issuing sheepish apologies to the dwarves we passed.

Marge's squad car led us across town and into a nice development of Spanish Mission style homes. She stopped at a side street and pulled over where a deputy's car was waiting. James parked the Jeep behind them, and we all got out.

"It's that one," Marge said, nodding at the one-story house at the very end of the street. "Deputy Franks is back at the station, watching over Allison, so it's just us four. Croft and Wesson, you're coming with me to the front. Rollie, I want you covering the back in case he tries to slip out."

Deputy Rollie, a portly man with a lampshade mustache,

nodded and trotted off while James and I followed the sheriff across the neat lawn.

"Hang back a little," she said as she stepped onto a front porch arranged with potted plants. She unholstered her revolver and banged loudly on the door. "Elmer? Vicki? It's Sheriff Jackson!"

The wind picked up, jingling a set of chimes. I nodded for James to be ready with an invocation. If Elmer was inside, we would need to drop him quickly, then find and destroy the idol before Gorr decided to pay him a visit. James nodded back, fist tight around his wand.

Marge banged on the door again. "It's Sheriff Jackson! I need you to open up!" She waited, then spoke into her shoulder radio. "Anything back there?"

"A few lights are on, but all the curtains are drawn," Rollie answered.

"Okay, keep watch. We're going in."

She tried the knob, then cocked her head for one of us to do the battering honors. I aimed my cane at the lock and spoke a force invocation. The bolt area coughed wood and the door slapped inward.

Marge swept the entrance with her firearm before nodding that it was clear. James and I followed her inside. Loud, clownish music was playing somewhere.

Marge quickly cleared the main rooms. A large flatscreen tuned to the Cartoon Network was on in the living room. When Marge turned it off, the house fell silent—except for sobbing from a room down the hallway.

James and I looked at one another, then followed Marge along a corridor lined with photos of Elmer and Vicki and what must have been their parents. The sobbing was coming from behind a closed door at the hallway's end. After clearing the other rooms, Marge signaled for us to stay back. She threw the door open and aimed the revolver inside with both hands.

"Don't move!" she ordered. "Hands behind your back!"

Someone shouted and then began to scream and struggle.

By the time I reached the room, Marge was already straddling Elmer, who was shirtless and face-down on a bed, fingers squirming at his low back. I drew my sword, but there was nothing to do. Marge snapped on the cuffs, then patted him down.

Not bad for a one-legged woman.

"Secure the rest of the house, then join us inside," Marge radioed Rollie. When she pushed herself off him, Elmer jerked and kicked, his screams falling to deep sobs.

"He's bleeding," James observed.

Marge rolled him onto his back. Elmer's face, already a wreck from crying, was pocked with bloody craters. Marge pulled away the bedsheet stuck to his chest. His torso was also bleeding.

Elmer flinched when James stepped forward. "Almost looks like gunshot wounds."

Marge wiped an especially messy crater in his right chest with a handkerchief and examined the wound. "Too superficial."

"That's because he didn't take the shots directly," I said. "Gorr did. Back in the cave."

James and Marge turned toward me, their faces competing for the more perplexed look.

"Elmer is bound to him," I explained. "He summoned Gorr with the idol, but Gorr must have needed a living connection to our plane. Whatever injuries Gorr suffers—eye gouges, rock-salt blasts, a tunnel collapsing over him—Elmer absorbs too, but with less intensity. Hence the weeping eye and superficial lesions."

He has to be in plenty of pain, though, I thought as he continued to sob, snot streaming from his nose. I wondered how he'd learned to use the idol, or if he'd any idea what he'd done.

"Elmer, where's the idol?" I asked firmly. "The little wooden man. Where is it?"

Elmer shook his head back and forth and began to babble. I looked around the room. Deputy Rollie appeared, and Marge ordered him to begin searching the house for the idol.

She then made a call on her phone. "Not answering," she muttered. "Elmer, where's your sister? Where's Vicki?"

That seemed to make Elmer sob harder.

"Oh, crap," I said, remembering the blond woman who had picked him up for lunch. "Gorr didn't get his sacrifice tonight. He may have demanded Vicki in Allison's stead."

"Vi-Vi-Vicki," Elmer babbled.

"No wonder he's so freaked out," James said.

"Here." I dug into a coat pocket and handed Marge a salt bag. "If you find the idol, throw it in the fireplace in the living room, pour this over it, and then light that sucker up. Its destruction will end this."

"Where are you going?" she asked.

"The mine. We need to reach Vicki before Gorr does."

"I can get us there in under ten," James said.

"Keep your phone on this time," Marge ordered. "And don't get your asses killed."

As Marge began searching the room, James and I left the house at a run. Even when we'd hit the street, I could still hear Elmer sobbing inside, babbling his sister's name over and over.

15

"So, what's our plan?" James asked above the roar of his engine.

"First, we find Vicki. The good news is that we know where she'll be. Which is also the bad news."

"You think Elmer slapped a bracelet on her?"

"Or she was compelled some other way," I said. "She's a little older than the other victims, but she looked like a natural blonde. Not the ideal tribute to Gorr, maybe, but close enough to appease him until the next full moon, I'm guessing. If we find her alive, we get her out."

"Not to crap on your parade, Prof, but we barely made it out ourselves the last time."

"How much explosive did you pack before we headed to the dwarves'?" I asked.

"Twenty pounds of magically-enhanced TNT."

"Enough to bring down another tunnel?"

"Enough to bring down half the mine."

"Good. While I go in for Vicki, can you booby-trap the escape route? Using a force invocation, I should be able to extract her from a distance. Gorr will never know we're there until I've got her."

"And when he gives chase..." James slapped the dashboard. "Boom. I like it."

"With any luck, Marge will find and destroy the idol before then. Gorr could be history before we even get there. In which case, it'll just be a matter of bringing Vicki back out and—"

Something slammed into the back right corner of the Jeep, sending it into a squalling fishtail. James swore and fought for control of the vehicle while I braced an arm against the dash. I thought about the TNT clunking around in the gun case and aimed my cane out the window.

As the Jeep tipped onto two wheels, I shouted, *"Vigore!"*

I didn't know how stable James's explosives were, and I didn't want to find out only after we'd been scattered halfway across the county. The force from my cane hit asphalt, knocking us back onto all four wheels and into a skidding series of spins. Smoke and dust billowed up around us as the Jeep jounced off the road and down into a basin of desert scrub.

A large rock slammed the undercarriage, and the Jeep came to a jarring halt.

"Dude," James said, giving his head a shake. "What the hell hit us?"

"That's what I'd like to know."

I peered out the windshield, past the Jeep's dim, dust-filled beams. As the world steadied, I saw our answer. Above the brush lining the roadside, rows of roof-mounted floodlights came into view: Santana's pack.

"Oh, not now," James moaned.

He cranked the ignition. The dead engine chugged but wouldn't turn over. He swore and pumped the gas pedal.

"Call Marge," I said. "Now."

James reached into his pocket and pulled out a shattered phone. "Crap. Must have smashed against the door when we went off road."

"Get to your weapons cache."

"They've only got lead in them."

"Then swap them out for silver. I'll hold off the wolves."

We both got out. As James hustled around to the back of the Jeep, I remained beside my closed door, squinting into the lights, watching the bushes for movement. The timing was shit, but we couldn't change that. We would have to deal with them as efficiently as possible.

"Oh, Jay-ames," Santana sang from off to the right.

I counted at least eight responding chuckles. The wolves were spread along the line of bushes, hard to pinpoint. I didn't like not being able to see them. With a whispered invocation, I grew out the light from my cane. When the orb enveloped me, the Jeep, and James, I hardened it into a protective shield.

"Sorry about that little collision back there," Santana said. "We sometimes forget to turn our lights on at night. Dampens our wolf vision, you know. And my driver is still learning. Has a habit of going through things instead of around them." The laughter from the other wolves was closer now.

"What's your excuse for my trailer?" James asked.

"No excuse," Santana replied. "That was just for shits and giggles, you know?"

"My dog was inside."

"Oh, dear, was she?" he asked in fake concern.

"Look ... I'm sorry about last night," James said. "I didn't mean to challenge you. My fear took over, and things got out of hand. Give me a week and I'll have your money. You'll never have to see my face again." Ammo clattered off the rear fender, and James swore under his breath.

Santana gave an exaggerated sniff. "Is that silver I smell?"

"Uh, no."

"If you're going to lie about that, hijo, how can I trust you to pay up?"

I could hear the growing edge in Santana's voice. He had no intention of letting James off the hook. Last night's insult had cut too deep. His only recourse was to end James as violently as possible, then eat his heart in front of his pack. I might be spared the "as violently as possible" part, but I was on the menu, too, just by dint of being in James's company. Sets of hungry eyes flashed on the verges of the Jeep's headlights. The pack was circling closer.

Dammit, we don't have time for this, I thought.

"Hey, James," I called. "Our plan for the mine?"

"Yeah...?"

I drew my cane into sword and staff. "Be ready."

It took a couple of seconds for what I was proposing to click. "But ... my Jeep," he said.

"Better your Jeep than our lives."

I aimed my blade at the closest pair of eyes and shouted a force invocation. The pulse shot through dust and brush and slammed into the wolf.

James opened fire with a lever-action rifle. Off to my right, a wolf bellowed in pain and skittered back. The remaining wolves crashed through the brush, their bulky forms moving with amazing speed. They'd gone full lupine, bloodlust on their faces. I incanted to reinforce the shield. They collided into it, their collective force shuddering through our protection.

I joined James at the back of the Jeep.

"Get them worked up," I said. "I'm going to do something with the shield. When I give the word, let her rip."

As the wolves attacked with battering lunges, snarling muzzles, and razor-sharp claws, I drew the shield smaller so that it was no longer around the Jeep—just James and me. With another invocation, I sent a pulse from the shield into the pack, dazzling them with light and knocking them back.

James took aim, his next shot tearing through the chest of the largest wolf. He dropped and went still, steam rising from the silver wound. But that only whipped the rest of the pack into a greater fury.

"Bring it on," I whispered, sidestepping from the Jeep.

As they charged back in, I flipped the shield from around me and James and enclosed the wolves with the vehicle.

"Now!" I called.

"Liberare!" James shouted.

The back of the Jeep exploded in a geyser that lifted the vehicle vertically and blew the wolves into fiery chunks. I grunted as the shield bowed out—the force like a sledgehammer blow in my head—then pulled the shield back around us before it could fail. The violent release of fire and pressure slammed into us, shooting us off like a pinball. A silver net manifested between a pair of pinyon pines, catching us and lowering us to the desert floor. Thoroughly spent, I dispersed the shield as James called the net invocation back into his wand.

"Holy crap," he said, blazing pieces of Jeep reflected in his eyes.

"C'mon," I said, limp-running toward the road. "We'll take one of their trucks. We have to get to the mine."

"I'm out of explosives," he pointed out.

"Then we'll improvise."

At the road, we chose one of the four trucks and climbed in. The cab smelled like oil, pot smoke, and wet animal. A skull keychain dangled from the ignition. James threw his rifle into the back seat and was reaching to turn the key when something ripped his door off its hinges. In a flash of hair, James was yanked from the cab and flung against a neighboring truck with a bang.

Crap, there was still a wolf out there, and I had a nasty feeling I knew which one.

I clambered out the passenger side and rounded the back of the truck, my sword sputtering with energy. I hadn't had enough time to recharge. James was on the ground, his brow bleeding, his right hand drawing his wand. But before he could manifest a protective shield, the werewolf flashed past again. In a burst of sparks, the wand somersaulted from James's grip.

"That wasn't my A team, or even my B team," Santana said.

I rounded toward his voice, but when he spoke again, it was off behind me.

"Just some *pinche* initiates, but they did their jobs as—how do you call it?—cannon fodder? If I can scrape them together and find someone decent at resurrection, maybe I'll promote them to full members." He chuckled savagely. "Give them your heads as trophies."

"Protezione," I uttered.

Light swelled from my staff, but when I went to harden it, the protective orb sputtered. Desperate, I called more energy.

Creamy waves lapped at the edges of my consciousness, meaning that if I pushed any harder, my incubus, Thelonious, would take over my body. And he was a lover, not a fighter.

I relented with a gasp and watched the light disappear.

"What's wrong?" Santana asked. "Shoot your load back there?"

James limped over, his Peacemakers drawn, and stood with his back to mine. I slid my staff through my belt and held my sword in both hands. We were both wielding silver. It was just a matter of getting a clean strike.

"I haven't tasted wizard in a long time," Santana taunted.

The wolf appeared in front of me, his tongue running over his gold-plated fangs. I thrust my sword, already knowing I was too slow. A hand crushed my right wrist and jerked me forward. The center of my face exploded in pain as a rock-solid fist met my nose.

James wheeled and fired a shot, but Santana had already darted out of range, his laughter cutting the air around us.

"You all right, man?" James asked above the ringing in my right ear.

"Only if I ignore the blood and pain," I replied stuffily. The first was spilling from my nose like a dribbling hose, and the second had become a savage throb that drove deep into my sinuses. I tested my nose cartilage with a finger and thumb. It felt loose.

"Dammit," James whispered, "I just need one decent—"

His guns exploded as Santana flashed past again. By the time I wheeled around, James was doubled over, and both his hands were empty. "Fucker gut-punched me and took my weapons."

"Not looking so good for you, is it?" Santana teased.

"Enough with the stick-and-move shit," James called. "Why don't you fight me like a man?"

Santana laughed. "I could've ripped your head off, then done the same to your friend before your body even hit the pavement. Is that what you want, hijo?"

I flinched as a large moth batted past on its way to the floodlights.

"You're not hearing me," James said. "You could do those things as a wolf, sure. I'm telling you to man up. Literally. Stop hiding behind the fur and fangs. Let's see what you've really got."

Santana would still have a huge advantage in strength and speed, but James was determined. My partner removed his vest and tossed it aside, shoved the sleeves of his gray tee up over his muscular shoulders, and pushed out his chest—all physical displays of challenge.

In the end, the Alpha couldn't resist.

Santana stepped from the shadows, his wolf form narrowing to the lean, tattooed physique of a notorious gang leader. His slender ponytail whipped as he cracked his neck viciously from side to side and flashed a gold smile. "A little space?" he said, signaling me back.

James nodded at me. I took several steps back but kept my sword raised.

"Ready to rumble, hijo?" Santana said, crouching slightly.

"Bring it, bitch."

Santana's smile hardened. He lunged forward, landing a vicious right to James's jaw. James staggered and swung a looping left. Santana ducked easily and landed a pair of blows to James's ribs. I grimaced at the sounds of bones cracking. Santana leaned away from a pair of reaching punches and then flashed back in with a straight left that knocked James against a truck.

"I thought you said we were gonna fight," Santana taunted.

"Dude." James paused to hawk a rag of blood. "Women have slapped me harder than that."

The insult crossed a final line. I could see in Santana's blazing eyes that he'd had enough, that he intended to finish James. I ran forward with the sword. Santana veered from his attack and blocked my strike, nearly breaking my forearm. The sword clattered to the asphalt. A kick to the stomach blew out my remaining air and splayed me onto my back.

Santana spun toward James—and then screamed in surprise.

James had pulled a dagger from his boot and driven it up beneath Santana's ribs. Judging from the burst of smoke, the blade held silver.

"How ya like me now?"

"Hijo de *puta!*" Santana hissed in his face.

"Never said I'd fight fair," James grunted, twisting the blade deeper.

Santana's scream was part human, part animal. He smashed his forehead into James's, knocking him to the ground. But Santana was in survival mode now. Blood gushed over his hands as he wrenched the dagger free and let it fall to the road. He staggered back, listing from side to side, and crashed through the bushes beside the road.

I retrieved my sword and stumbled after him, but James caught my arm.

"He's still dangerous," he said. "And we've gotta get our butts to the mine."

He was right. James recovered his wand, and we climbed

back into the truck. The engine started with a roar. Cold wind blasted through the cab as James accelerated away.

I brought a sleeve to my raw, busted nose, then peered over at my partner. We looked like we'd been run over. I tuned into my mental prism. My magic was in the beginning stages of recharging, but it would be far short of maximum power by the time we reached the mine.

"Hope to hell Marge found the idol," James said, echoing my own thoughts.

16

James gunned the truck up the dirt road into Rattlesnake Hills until we were pulling onto the stone shelf. As the powerful lights swept over the parked vehicles beneath the overhang, the white sports car Vicki had been driving earlier flashed into view.

"She's here," I said, already throwing my door open.

James grabbed the rifle from the back seat and jumped out his side. We ran up the steps to the mine, James sending an illumination orb ahead. At the entrance, I took quick stock of the sand. Over our earlier footprints were two messy lines, as though Vicki had scuffed her way inside.

The thought of returning underground made my chest squeeze around my racing heart, but my phobia would have to wait. We found the shaft and descended the ladder quickly, our panting breaths echoing off the rock walls. I noticed a rope running among the cables that ran beside the ladder but couldn't remember whether it had been there the last time.

When we arrived at the side tunnel, I dug into my coat pockets until I felt the bracelet. I withdrew it carefully, amazed it hadn't fallen out during our various conflicts. It pulsed darkly, communicating with its twin: the bracelet perched on the pagan cross in the killing chamber.

"Think Vicki made it past the section we blew?" James asked.

"More likely the bracelet led her down an alternate route."

We followed the ore-cart tracks. Sure enough, before we reached the collapse, the bracelet pulled toward a tunnel on our right. I stopped to listen. Hearing nothing, I looked back at James. His face was bloody, his right cheek shiny with swelling. I'd considered administering some healing magic to us on the ride here, but I needed to conserve my still-depleted power.

"This is where we're gonna split," I decided.

"Screw that, man," James whispered. "We're sticking together."

"No, listen to me. If Gorr is down there, we don't have anything in our arsenal right now that can slow or hurt him. I need you to search the other tunnels, see if you can find any more old dynamite. Then get back here, mine this tunnel, and wait for me. We'll do what we did the last time." Only this time, I hoped I'd have one of the victims with me, alive.

"All right, Prof. But be careful."

"Yeah, you too."

Before I could turn away, James gripped my hand and pulled me into a one-armed hug. He didn't say anything and didn't have to. We'd grown a lot closer in the last few hours. He clapped my back, then released me. As he and his illumination orb returned the way we'd come, I called the barest light to my staff and headed down the new tunnel.

The curving passage was narrower than the one I'd left.

Small cave-ins littered the floor, and in several of them I could see the scuff lines I'd observed at the mine's entrance. That gave me hope that Vicki had arrived here slowly. That there was still time.

Without warning, the passage turned sharply, and a smell of decomposition hit me in the face. I stifled a gag and killed my light. I was staring into the killing chamber. By the faint moonlight, I could make out a body in front of the altar. The woman appeared to be on her knees, torso thrown forward in a child's pose. Blond hair spilled over her extended arms.

It was Vicki, but I couldn't tell whether she was alive.

I scanned the chamber. It was darker than when we'd been here earlier, harder to see into the various recesses. I opened my senses now. Black, tarry energy coursed throughout the room, but I couldn't feel it concentrating anywhere. As far as I could tell, Gorr wasn't here.

Destroyed?

Setting the bracelet on the tunnel floor, I reached into a coat pocket for my spare salt bag, which had torn open at some point. Digging out part of the spill from my pocket, I sprinkled a protective circle around the bracelet to blunt its signal to Gorr.

"Vicki," I whispered, looking around as I paced toward her.

The altar I'd crash-landed on earlier had been restored, I saw. The urns righted, their macabre contents cleaned up. The cross had been straightened, too, the twin bracelet hanging on the crux.

"Vicki," I whispered a little more loudly.

This time she shifted. I considered using a force invocation to pull her toward me, but I didn't know what kind of an enchantment might be holding her there. I hustled the remaining distance and placed a hand on her back. She was warm beneath her thin leather jacket. Hot, even. Meaning she was still with us. From beneath her hair, I could hear her murmuring in a whisper, probably in the thrall of another bracelet. But when I felt both of her wrists, they were bare.

Wrapping a hand around her side, I whispered, "Vicki. We need to get out of here."

She jerked and turned her head. Through her hair, I could see the shine of her right eye.

Behind me, something scuffed over the stone floor. I twisted my torso around, heart in my throat. But the cavern was empty. A metallic clink accompanied the next scuff. I trained my gaze lower.

Shit.

The bracelet had broken through my protective circle and was inching its way toward the altar. On the cross, the other bracelet began to rattle. A jarring resonance took up between the twin bracelets, ringing deep in my ears and causing the energy in the room to swirl.

"The bracelet is a more effective signal than prayer."

When I turned back, Vicki had risen to her feet, her blond hair fluttering in the gathering storm of energy. Above her smiling lips, her dark eyes glinted fiercely. "Thank you for delivering it to us."

Wait, what?

My eyes fell down her neck to where an old wooden idol dangled.

A violent charge went off in my chest. Vicki wasn't a victim but the perpetrator. That's what Elmer had wanted to tell us back at the house, but he'd been too upset to get the words out.

Absent the bracelet, Vicki had been attempting to

summon Gorr through prayer just now. But to claim whom? My eyes cut toward a figure in the shadows behind the altar. I pushed more light from my staff until blond hair and a pink sweater emerged from the darkness.

Allison?

"Gorr had his appetite set on her," Vicki said. "Fortunately, Deputy Franks isn't much of a watchdog. I found him sacked out, as Gorr said I would."

I remembered the home remedy the deputy had told Marge he was taking for his sore throat. The alcohol must have put him to sleep.

"The hard part was getting the unconscious tribute down here," she said.

Of course. The dragging tracks in the sand, the rope hanging down the incline shaft…

"Vigore!" I shouted, aiming my blade at the idol and jerking it back. The invocation tunneled weakly through the thickening energy in the cavern, tugging the idol, but failing to snap the cord that secured it around Vicki's neck. Vicki staggered forward but regained her footing. Placing a hand over the idol, she pressed it protectively to her chest and stared past me.

"He means to destroy you," she called. "Kill him."

I wheeled around to find Gorr growing from the dark energy. The zombie god with his tangled hair, staring, caul-covered eyes, and tattered robes, hardened into form.

I threw up a protective shield an instant before he swiped an arm toward me. His fist exploded through the manifestation, knocking me from the shrine and onto my back. When I squinted up, he was staring down at me from across the chamber, Vicki safely behind him.

"Your brother," I grunted, gaining my feet. "How could

you bind him, of all people, to this monstrosity? He's at home right now, bleeding and screaming in pain. Did you know that?"

"This is for him as much as anyone," she said.

"No one calls Gorr out of altruism. It takes a special kind of greed. Judging from your car and clothes, not to mention your obvious surgical enhancements, you blow through a lot of money. What happened? Did the credit card companies threaten to cut off your lines? Were the loan sharks circling?"

I sidestepped at a cautious distance as I spoke, waiting for Gorr to make a move so I could get another play at the idol. But he remained close to Vicki, shielding her with his massive form.

Vicki's voice became defensive. "What my parents left me when they died wasn't enough to take care of Elmer."

"So you put him to work in the lots, probably the only place that would employ him, figuring he could help pay for his own care. Meanwhile, you spent the inheritance on yourself." I could hear her breathing speed up. "Somewhere in there, you found the idol among your father's possessions. Maybe in a trunk with some old photos and letters, relics from his side of the family. The bracelets too. You learned what they were and how to activate them. After binding your brother to Gorr, you targeted his first victim, who happened to work at the lot: Dawn Michaels. A young woman you didn't think anyone would miss. You led her here—to Sten's old mine—for Gorr to consume. And for what? Some gold?"

"Shut up," Vicki said.

"That's when you learned the girls at the lot were protected. Knowing it was too risky to pluck from their ranks again, you set your sights on easier targets—innocent young women you scouted out during your social work rounds."

"Shut up!" she screamed.

"Maybe somewhere along the line you decided you'd amassed enough riches. But Gorr wasn't ready to stop, was he? He'd developed a taste for the sacrifices, each one making him hungrier for the next. He threatened your life on the next full moon, and the show went on."

"Make him shut up!" Vicki screamed at Gorr, giving him a two-handed shove from behind.

Gorr plodded forward. I cut one way, then the other, looking for an opening, but the zombie god kept himself between me and the idol that animated him. I backpedaled. If he seized me, it would be over. No one would know she was the perp, not even James. By the time my partner came looking for me, Allison and I would be dead, Gorr would have returned to his realm, and Vicki would have had time to concoct a story, one James might not be able to see through. She would pin it on her brother, paint herself as the victim. While her brother was being processed, she would split town with the idol and bracelets.

I couldn't let that happen.

"Vigore!" I called, thrusting my sword forward.

But instead of directing the force at Gorr or Vicki, I hooked it around Allison's ankle and dragged her from behind the altar. Even that simple invocation was draining, but it had the desired effect. Gorr halted his advance toward me and turned his head toward his offering, which was sliding away. I sensed the hunger churning inside him. He changed course, stalking toward Allison.

"Hey, come back here!" Vicki cried.

Her right hand was still clamping the idol to her chest. The other was stretched toward Gorr, trying to command him. I didn't have the power to pull the idol free, not from this distance. And I wouldn't be able to cross the chamber on foot before Gorr retrieved Allison and returned to protect Vicki.

Metal rang against stone. I looked over to see the bracelet that had been making its way across the floor arrive at the base of the shrine's cross. It jittered excitedly beneath its twin.

And then there's Option C, I thought.

Shaping a force invocation, I released it. The bracelet sprang from the floor and shot onto Vicki's outstretched hand. *Gotcha!*

She cried out as the energy clamped her wrist and began squirming up her arm.

Gorr stopped advancing on Allison and spun toward Vicki. A hungry moan seeped from his lips.

"No," Vicki said, trying desperately to pry the bracelet off herself as she backed away. "I'm not the tribute. *She's* the tribute. I-I'm your master. I command you to protect me."

Gorr's posture sagged as he stopped in front of her.

"That's better," she said. "Now I want you to—"

Gorr seized her around the waist and lifted her toward his mouth.

"No!" she shouted, kicking her legs. "Release me!"

Gorr's bloated lips parted, ropes of saliva stretching between his teeth.

"No! No! No!" Vicki shrieked. "God dammit, *nooo!*"

I cringed, unable to look. But I couldn't block out the crunching and gnawing or Vicki's death cries. When at last I peeked, Gorr was stumbling drunkenly, tearing his victim's remains apart in ecstatic spasms. I was going to need counseling, but first I needed to finish this.

When Sten Klausen had failed to deliver a sacrifice to Gorr more than a hundred years ago, the zombie god had strangled the life from him. Without a male mortal binding him to our plane, Gorr had returned to the underworld. But in the present case, Gorr was bound to Elmer, not Vicki. He would persist here as long as Elmer did—or the idol. My eyes searched the floor until I spotted the wooden figure half buried in gore.

"*Vigore!*" I called, snagging it with a weak force invocation.

The idol kicked and then began skidding toward me. Seeing what was happening, Gorr dropped Vicki's remains and ran until he was gaining on the idol. I dashed toward the idol from the other direction, digging into the pockets of my flapping coat to locate the vial I would need to torch the wooden figure.

I reached the idol a second before Gorr. Like a runner in a shuttle race, I planted my front leg, grasped the blood-soaked idol, and pushed myself into a sprint in the other direction. If James had managed to locate some explosives, we would replay the last escape, only this time we'd salt and burn the idol, destroying Gorr, and then come back for Allison.

I was almost clear of the killing chamber when Gorr's fingers hooked the back of my coat. I tried to shed it, even if that meant losing my salt and dragon sand, but Gorr's other hand was already around me, pinning an arm to my side and crushing the air from my lungs. Grunting, I curled the fingers of my free hand around the idol and tried to snap it against my chest, but the wood was too dense.

"*Respingere,*" I grunted.

Power flashed from the coin pendant around my neck, but it didn't affect Gorr. His lips parted as he lifted me, releasing the stink of a mass grave. Between his rotting teeth, I could see shreds of Vicki's designer jacket.

I kicked desperately, managing to plant a foot against Gorr's throat and the other below his nose. I wasn't going to end up like Vicki. Wasn't going to allow Allison to be next. Wasn't going to let this monstrosity roam free.

Gorr moaned and knocked my leg down with his other hand. With my final reserves, I redoubled my efforts to snap the idol. I could feel my breastbone bruising, but the damned wood would not give.

Someone whistled. "Everson, the idol!"

I squinted over to where James had entered the chamber. He clapped twice and showed me his hands. With a grunt, I shot-putted the idol toward him. He bent low to catch it and then waved it overhead.

"Hey, Smelly! Look what I've got!"

With a groan, Gorr closed his mouth and dropped me. I landed hard, my body one gigantic throb, but I understood James's plan. While he danced back from Gorr, I struggled to my feet, uncapped the vial of dragon sand in one coat pocket and dug out a small handful of salt from another. The instant before Gorr grabbed him, James slid the idol toward me.

"Smoke that bitch!" James yelled.

With a foot, I trapped the idol and dumped the salt and dragon sand over it.

Gorr wheeled toward me and charged. I had just enough time to jump back and shout, *"Fuoco!"*

The dragon sand ignited with a dark red burst that swallowed the idol. Gorr arrived over it and tried to stomp it out as his own body erupted into a flurry of blue fire. He staggered back and slapped at the spreading flames. They turned orange, then a fierce red, climbing up into his tangled hair. The milky cauls bubbled and dripped from his eyes. When he tried to moan, fire jetted from his throat, choking off the sound. His insides were burning now.

James limped to my side, a hand bracing the right side of his ribs.

Safely back, we watched Gorr's form stiffen to a charcoal-like blackness. At last, he toppled backwards, still flickering, and burst against the cavern floor, just a larger version of the idol's ashes at my feet.

James clapped my shoulder as the last of the cavern's dark energy dissipated. "So that's what happens when you kill a god, huh?"

"Damned straight," I said, releasing my breath. "And guess who was behind him?" I filled James in quickly as we crossed the chamber to check on Allison, who was starting to come to.

"Vicki," James repeated, shaking his head. "And just this morning I'd been thinking I might want her number. Oh, hey," he whispered, placing a hand on my chest. "Mind if I do the hero thing solo?"

I glanced from Allison to him. "Why not both of us?"

"No offense, but you're not much to look at right now."

"*I'm* not much to look at? Have you seen your face lately?"

"I imagine it's as bad as it feels, but yours looks like a baboon's ass that's been kicked really hard."

Despite everything, the absurd image made me snuff out a laugh that killed my broken nose.

James gave me a companionable nudge. "You can play hero next time."

I narrowed my swollen eyes at him, but what could I say? My partner's timing *had* saved my life, not to mention helping destroy a god and close a dangerous portal to the nether realms.

I relented. "Go get her, cowboy."

17

After taking James's and my accounts, speaking with Elmer, and performing a thorough search of Vicki's records and property, Marge and the Grimstone County Sheriff's Department wrapped up their investigation that week.

Vicki's late mother had spent her final years researching the family's genealogy. She was the one who had discovered the idol and bracelets in a box of her husband's family's old things. The box also contained a small leather-bound journal in which Sten Klausen detailed the rites he'd used to call Gorr, and how, as a result, he'd started paying down his debts.

Vicki's mother had concluded in her notes about Sten Klausen that the man was "batshit crazy." She hadn't believed any of it. When she died, though, those notes went to Vicki.

I had been right about Vicki's finances. With her compulsive spending habits, she'd amassed a sizeable debt. About a quarter million dollars' worth. Yeah. Those surgeries weren't cheap.

When shady collectors began pounding on the door,

Vicki might have remembered her mother mentioning a crazy great-great-grandfather who claimed to have made sacrifices to a god in exchange for gold. At that point, Vicki would have tried anything. And she had what she needed: the idol, the bracelets, the instructions, and access to the old shrine.

She'd made an arrangement with a buyer for the gold, which, due to high demand, was selling at a premium. Within five months, Vicki's debts were paid, plus interest. It appeared she *did* try to quit, but as Sten Klausen learned the hard way, once Gorr got going, he didn't like to stop.

On a related note, Taffy eventually told Marge that he'd purchased Sten's claim at the 1902 auction after seeing what the man had been pulling from his mine. He'd been mystified when, after two years and an extensive operation, the dwarves had produced diddlysquat from the same claim. Of course, they hadn't had a Norse god of wealth to lean on.

In Vicki's case, she found Gorr another sacrifice just in time, sparing herself Sten's fate. Five murders became six and then seven. More and more gold fell into her blood-stained lap. In the last few months, she had been scrambling to spread her money across a variety of accounts to avoid suspicion.

She wouldn't have to worry about that anymore.

As for the victims, their remains were exhumed from the mine to receive proper burials, including the two women who had disappeared during Sten's time, their disappearances no longer a mystery.

With the case solved and the god destroyed, there had been nothing left for James and me to do but clean the bracelets and pack them in salt for delivery to our order.

Naturally, we received commendations from the Grimstone County Sheriff's Department for our crack work.

Sort of...

"Man, this is for the birds," James complained. Straightening from his mop, he squinted at the swath of tar we'd smeared over half the sheriff department's rooftop. As punishment for disobeying her orders, not to mention riling up the dwarves, Marge had sentenced us to a long weekend of manual labor.

"Oh, a little non-magical work never killed anyone," I said.

"No, but these god-awful fumes might. Feels like they're sticking to my lungs."

"Then invoke a filter. Hey, you missed a spot over there."

"Where?"

I showed him with a jutted chin. Grumbling, James slapped some tar over it.

"You know we're up here because of you, don't you?" he said.

"Yeah, well, at least I get into the kind of trouble I can get back out of."

"You referring to the werewolves?"

There had been no word from Santana since the night James stabbed him. By all accounts he'd disappeared, meaning he was either out in the desert, his bones being picked over by carrion birds, or he'd gone into hiding until he healed. I had a nasty feeling it was the second. To be safe, James and I had spent the last few nights strengthening the trailer's defensive wards.

"*And* the witch," I reminded him. "Madam Helga isn't going to forget that favor you owe her."

"Even though we killed the dude that grabbed her girl?"

"Nope."

"That's messed up, man. Well, the dwarves are all on you."

I couldn't argue with him there. Dwarves were famous for holding grudges. We pushed our black mops around, the tar's fumes rising past us while the afternoon sun beat down on our bare backs.

"While you were meeting with the insurance agent about your trailer this morning," I said, "I gave my report to the Order."

James looked over at me. "And...?"

"And I told them what happened."

"Everything?" he asked nervously.

I nodded. "Of course, I described the werewolf attacks as unprovoked," I added with a grin.

James's shoulders relaxed. "Thanks, bro."

"Hey, you kept up your end of the deal: You took the case seriously. You got us the lead on the bracelet, which was huge. And there's no way I would have been able to stop Gorr if you hadn't been there. More likely, I'd still be down in that mine—in pieces. Anyway, I told all of that to the Order. They sounded pleased." I stopped to lean on my mop. "Look, I wasn't too excited about coming out here and playing mentor when I probably need as much mentoring as anyone. But we actually made a pretty competent team."

"Aw, man, you're making me misty eyed."

"Which is good," I went on, "because the Order said I could be sent out here again. I hope that doesn't crimp your style."

"Just so long as we don't have to tar any more rooftops."

"I'll try to be better."

He smirked. "Then so will I, Prof. Mop-shake on it?"

James held out his dripping mop. I laughed and tapped it with the end of mine. "Oh, I almost forgot," I said. "The Order's going to reimburse you for the damage to your trailer and Jeep, also for your lost firearms."

He broke into a huge smile. "Now that's gonna make me cry for real."

"Thought you might like that."

"Sh-sheriff says you can c-come down now!" a voice called up.

James and I walked to the edge of the roof and peered down at Elmer's upturned face. With the idol destroyed, the bonding spell had released him, and Elmer had responded well to my healing magic. Within days he was asking about going back to work. Though his sister had stuck him in the lot for selfish reasons, it turned out Elmer enjoyed the employment.

Marge set him up with a couple odd jobs around town, including lawn maintenance for the sheriff's department. And since there were no protocols for seizing money obtained through a god, Vicky's accounts were transferred to a fund for Elmer, which allowed him to stay in his house and paid for a fulltime caregiver. Given his devotion to protecting women, something told me the victims would have been okay with that.

"Thanks, big man," James called down, giving him a thumb's up.

Elmer removed his cupped hand from his brow and returned the gesture enthusiastically before hustling off.

"Well," I said, grabbing my shirt from the top of an unopened tar bucket, "guess I've got a plane to catch."

"Oh, hey, would you mind too much taking a cab to the airport?" James asked.

"You can't drive me in your rental?"

"I've got another date with Allison."

"You're ditching your partner?"

"Hey, I'd ditch Merlin himself for the right woman."

"Fair enough. I guess. So, it sounds like she's doing all right?"

"She's awesome," James said, smiling a little too broadly.

"I don't want to know what that means, do I?"

"No, you don't, Prof."

I shook my head. Laughing, James clapped my shoulders and held the ladder for me to climb down.

The End

But Croft & Wesson's adventures have only begun. Keep reading to learn more...

GRIMSTONE HANGOVER
CROFT & WESSON 2

A case they'll never forget… if only they can remember.

Professor Croft here, partnered once again with the gambling, spell-slinging James Wesson.

Four Grimstone teens are dead, the life seemingly vacuumed from their withered bodies. The lone clue, a magic residue in their blood. Convinced it's the work of a supernatural drug, Sheriff Jackson entrusts the case to us while she's away. I just need to keep my junior partner in line.

Suddenly it's the next morning, and we're hungover, absent our magical items, and with no memory of the last twelve hours. Were we drugged? James keeps bringing up some movie, but I'm desperately trying to piece together what happened. Because the more we discover about our wild night, the less innocent we seem. And the deputy is missing.

Can we undo the damage, find the deputy, and crack the case before Sheriff Jackson returns to town?

Or will the wizard duo of Croft and Wesson become Grimstone's next outlaws?

AVAILABLE NOW!

Grimstone Hangover
(Croft & Wesson, Book 2)

AUTHOR'S NOTE

Croft & Wesson is a spinoff of my long-running *Prof Croft* series.

It was written as a standalone, but if you're new to the world and want to read more, start with *Book of Souls: A Prof Croft Prequel Novella.* That's where it all begins for Prof Croft. And it leads right into the main series, where he eventually meets fellow spell-slinger James Wesson.

What's ahead for these two? More adventures in Grimstone, County of course. Madam Helga still has an errand for James, after all, and we never did learn what became of the werewolf Santana. That said, there's no limit to what can happen when these two get together. That's no truer than in the next installment, *Grimstone Hangover*, available now.

I want to extend my special thanks to Matt Abraham for organizing the *Eight in the Chamber* box set in which this story originally appeared as *Croft and Wesson*; to Deranged Doctor Design for another stellar cover design; to Myra Shelley for her editing; and to Sharlene Magnarella for final proofing. Naturally, any errors or inelegance that remain are this author's alone.

To keep up with future releases, be sure to sign up to my newsletter. As a thank you, I'll also send you a pair of Prof Croft ebook novellas, including a subscriber exclusive that tells the story of how Everson Croft met his talking cat.

You can sign up at bradmagnarella.com

I do hope you'll stick around, partner.

Best wishes,
Brad Magnarella

CROFTVERSE CATALOGUE

PROF CROFT PREQUELS

Book of Souls

Siren Call

MAIN SERIES

Demon Moon

Blood Deal

Purge City

Death Mage

Black Luck

Power Game

Druid Bond

Night Rune

Shadow Duel

Shadow Deep

Godly Wars

Angel Doom

SPIN-OFFS

Croft & Tabby

Croft & Wesson

BLUE WOLF

Blue Curse

Blue Shadow

Blue Howl

Blue Venom

Blue Blood

Blue Storm

SPIN-OFF

Legion Files

For the entire chronology go to bradmagnarella.com

ABOUT THE AUTHOR

Brad Magnarella writes urban fantasy for the same reason most read it…

To explore worlds where magic crackles from fingertips, vampires and shifters walk city streets, cats talk (some excessively), and good prevails against all odds. It's shamelessly fun.

His two main series, Prof Croft and Blue Wolf, make up the growing Croftverse, with over a quarter-million books sold to date and an Independent Audiobook Award nomination.

Hopelessly nomadic, Brad can be found in a rented room overseas or hiking America's backcountry.

Or just go to www.bradmagnarella.com

Printed in Great Britain
by Amazon